Highlander Honored

Rebellious Highland Hearts
Book Two

JAYNE
CASTEL

WINTER MIST
PRESS

***

To a wonderful, loyal reader, Kay C.

***

Can a woman who is r
a man who believes in
A disgraced laird's dau
charged with protectir
desire, and courage in ....

After a love affair turns into tragedy, Davina Campbell seeks to escape her life at Kilchurn Castle and her father's domineering ways. She won't marry any of the men he keeps pushing at her—instead, she will take the veil and make a fresh start. But the man who leads her escort both infuriates and intrigues her, rousing a dangerous passion.

Restless, arrogant, and a touch cynical, Lennox Mackay has left his family behind to take up a new position as Captain of the Kilchurn Guard. However, five months into his new role, he's charged with escorting the laird's troublesome daughter to a nunnery.

The task sounds straightforward, yet it turns out not to be. And when their journey leads them into trouble, Davina and Lennox's fates become entwined.

Before leaving Kilchurn, they were both lost and restless—but could each be what the other is looking for?

Rebellious Highland Hearts is a four-book series following Iver Mackay of Dun Ugadale and his three brothers—Lennox, Kerr, and Brodie—as they meet women who will change their lives forever.

Historical Romances by Jayne Castel

DARK AGES BRITAIN

The Kingdom of the East Angles series
Night Shadows (prequel novella)
Dark Under the Cover of Night (Book One)
Nightfall till Daybreak (Book Two)
The Deepening Night (Book Three)
The Kingdom of the East Angles: The Complete Series

The Kingdom of Mercia series
The Breaking Dawn (Book One)
Darkest before Dawn (Book Two)
Dawn of Wolves (Book Three)
The Kingdom of Mercia: The Complete Series

The Kingdom of Northumbria series
The Whispering Wind (Book One)
Wind Song (Book Two)
Lord of the North Wind (Book Three)
The Kingdom of Northumbria: The Complete Series

DARK AGES SCOTLAND

The Warrior Brothers of Skye series
Blood Feud (Book One)
Barbarian Slave (Book Two)
Battle Eagle (Book Three)
The Warrior Brothers of Skye: The Complete Series

The Pict Wars series
Warrior's Heart (Book One)
Warrior's Secret (Book Two)
Warrior's Wrath (Book Three)
The Pict Wars: The Complete Series

On the Empire's Edge Duology

Taming the Eagle
Ensnaring the Dove

Novellas
Winter's Promise

MEDIEVAL SCOTLAND

The Brides of Skye series
The Beast's Bride (Book One)
The Outlaw's Bride (Book Two)
The Rogue's Bride (Book Three)
The Brides of Skye: The Complete Series

The Sisters of Kilbride series
Unforgotten (Book One)
Awoken (Book Two)
Fallen (Book Three)
Claimed (Epilogue novella)
The Sisters of Kilbride: The Complete Series

The Immortal Highland Centurions series
Maximus (Book One)
Cassian (Book Two)
Draco (Book Three)
The Laird's Return (Epilogue festive novella)
The Immortal Highland Centurions: The Complete Series

Guardians of Alba series
Nessa's Seduction (Book One)
Fyfa's Sacrifice (Book Two)
Breanna's Surrender (Book Three)
Guardians of Alba: The Complete Series

Stolen Highland Hearts series
Highlander Deceived (Book One)
Highlander Entangled (Book Two)
Highlander Forbidden (Book Three)
Highlander Pledged (Book Four)

Courageous Highland Hearts series
Highlander Defied (Book One)
Highlander Tempted (Book Two)
Highlander Healed (Book Three)
Highlander Sworn (Book Four)

Rebellious Highland Hearts series
Highlander Seduced (Book One)
Highlander Honored (Book Two)

Epic Fantasy Romances by Jayne Castel

Light and Darkness series
Ruled by Shadows (Book One)
The Lost Swallow (Book Two)
Path of the Dark (Book Three)
Light and Darkness: The Complete Series

*"They say a person needs just three things
to be truly happy in this world:
someone to love,
something to do,
and something to hope for."*
—Tom Bodett

1: YE WILL DO YER DUTY

Kilchurn Castle
Argyll, Scotland

July, 1453

THE LAIRD AND his daughter often argued—yet this evening, their squabbling was different. Tonight, blood was about to be spilled.

Seated at the long table upon the dais, Lennox swirled his goblet of wine gently as he listened to Colin and Davina Campbell snarl at each other from opposite sides of the table.

"Ewan Stewart is a worthy match, lass," Campbell ground out. "Ye will *not* refuse him like ye have done the others."

"I will," Davina shot back, her grey-blue eyes hardening. "I've told ye a thousand times. I've no interest in taking a husband. Not anymore. I just wish to be left alone."

Campbell slammed his goblet down on the table, sloshing dark wine over the rim. "Enough of this nonsense!" he bellowed, his temper snapping. His face was the color of liver now. "Ye will do yer duty!"

Lennox's gaze narrowed. In the five months he'd served Campbell, he'd never seen him so worked up. Aye, he'd tried to marry his errant daughter off a few times, yet when she refused, he'd let the matter drop.

But not tonight.

Of course, Lennox knew why. Ewan Stewart was a powerful laird and close relative to King James. It was the alliance Campbell craved, yet his daughter was proving frustratingly obstinate.

"I will not!" Davina drew herself up in outrage. High spots of color marked her wan cheeks, and her gaze burned. Her slender frame trembled with rage. "Ye will have to drag me to the chapel in chains, for I will never go willingly!"

"Don't test me, Davina." Colin Campbell launched himself to his feet then, spittle flying as he planted his large hands on the table between them and loomed over his daughter. "Look at ye. I used to be proud of my daughter ... yet I barely recognize the lass before me now." Davina flinched, her throat bobbing. But her father hadn't finished. "Ye have turned into a mewling scold. I tire of seeing ye drifting about this tower house like a tragic wraith. With yer mother gone, ye are chatelaine of Kilchurn, yet ye barely leave yer solar. Ye are little use to me as it is, but yer refusal to wed has turned ye into a millstone around my neck."

Tilting up her elfin face, Davina held her father's gaze, a muscle feathering in her jaw. "Then send me away," she whispered. "All I do is cause trouble here."

"This is my fault," he growled back. "Yer mother warned me once that I indulged ye overly ... that I gave ye too much freedom. Perhaps if I'd been stricter, ye wouldn't have disgraced yerself with Cameron."

Lennox lifted his goblet to his lips and took a sip. The laird wasn't holding himself back this eve. Nonetheless, there wasn't a soul in this keep who didn't know about the scandal that had befallen his daughter. It had happened well over six months before Lennox's arrival at Kilchurn, yet many of the servants still whispered about the fateful day.

He swallowed his mouthful of wine. It tasted vinegary this eve, although perhaps it was the atmosphere in the hall that soured it. Curse Campbell and his willful daughter. After a grueling day training recruits—for, with the growing unrest between the Stewarts and the

Douglases, the laird wanted Kilchurn's defenses strengthened—Lennox had been looking forward to a hearty supper and good wine. His role was draining, and there were times when he wished he could take his meals, alone, in his bedchamber. Just to get some peace.

Some of Campbell's men-at-arms sat at the long trestle tables below. Like Lennox, they'd been tucking into their blood sausage and coarse oaten bread before the argument erupted. Now all eyes were on the laird and his daughter.

"Ye didn't have to kill him," Davina replied between gritted teeth. Her slender frame trembled now, even as her gaze burned.

"Cameron overstepped," Campbell choked out. "He was far beneath ye. Ye are the daughter of the Lord of Glenorchy ... ye must make a worthy match."

"No!" she cried, her voice cracking as emotion overwhelmed her. Tears spilled over then, trickling down her cheeks. "Just leave me be!"

Lennox tensed, setting his goblet down on the table next to his unfinished supper. He hadn't seen the laird's daughter weep before. Often, a woman's tears left him unmoved. In his experience, they were used to manipulate their menfolk. But not in this case. Davina's unhappiness, her desperation, rippled across the table— as did her fury.

Nonetheless, irritation bubbled up within him.

God's teeth. Couldn't the troublesome woman give her father what he wanted so everyone else could have some peace?

"Send me to Iona as I've asked, and let us be done with this," she continued, her voice cracking, "for ye shall never bend me to yer will."

"Insolent chit!" Campbell's hand lashed out, his palm colliding with Davina's cheek. "Ye *will* obey me!"

Crying out, she reeled back, tumbling off the low bench where she sat.

In an instant, Lennox was on his feet and at her side, helping her up.

Lord, she was frail. It was like picking up a bird—one with alabaster skin and a mane of ebony hair that was presently in disarray.

But, despite the red welt that had now flamed upon her cheek, the fire in her eyes hadn't dimmed.

Extricating herself from his grip, she cast him a baleful look. Of course, he was Campbell's man. She didn't trust him. Stepping away from Lennox, she faced her father once more.

Yet when Lennox's gaze traveled to the laird, he saw a change had come over the man.

Colin Campbell now sat slumped at the table. His bearded face had sagged, and his blue-grey eyes—the same hue as his daughter's—glittered with tears.

The man wasn't in the habit of hitting his daughter, and his own loss of control had shocked him. "Why are ye determined to turn me into a beast, lass?" he rasped.

"I'm not," Davina replied roughly. "Ye have done that entirely without my assistance."

Their stare drew out, and pain flickered across Campbell's face.

Lennox observed the duel. The man could be a boor at times, yet Lennox usually got on well with him. All the same, the laird had made a right mess of things with his daughter. It was a situation that would never likely be resolved—and as the moments passed, realization dawned in Campbell's eyes.

"Very well," the laird replied after a long pause. "Take the veil. I cannot have a disobedient daughter living in my keep." His mouth twisted then. "I pity the nuns at Iona though ... for ye are difficult and lack piety." Davina's eyes snapped wide, and her lips parted as she started to respond. However, he hadn't yet finished. "But know this, Davina. If ye ride away from Kilchurn, there will be no returning. If ye choose to become a nun instead of wedding Ewan Stewart, ye will be dead to me."

Lennox stilled. That was harsh.

Even in defeat, Campbell wouldn't be defied.

Davina stared back at him, her slight frame quivering. "I understand," she replied huskily.

"Very well." Her father glanced away. "Go on ... return to yer bower, and pack yer things. Ye leave at first light."

Wordlessly, Davina stepped down from the dais and left the hall, her slippered feet whispering on the oak floorboards.

Silence settled over the cavernous space in the aftermath. Those gathered inside the hall hadn't resumed eating their suppers after witnessing the scene. Indeed, it appeared to have robbed them all of appetite.

Likewise, Lennox didn't feel like finishing his meal. Instead, he returned to his seat and picked up his goblet of wine, draining its contents in one draft before refilling it from a ewer in front of him.

A few feet away, Campbell sat staring down at his hands.

His expression was shuttered, yet his gaze glittered.

He'd refused to back down, and in doing so had lost his daughter.

And despite that Lennox was inclined to think the man was a stubborn mule, pity for the laird tugged at him as well. It seemed Campbell loved his daughter, even in her disgrace, yet he had just turned his back on her.

All the same, Lennox was grateful to finally have some peace—even if the nasty scene had spoiled his appetite. A pity too, as he'd been enjoying the blood sausage.

Feeling the weight of his captain's stare, the laird's gaze shifted right, spearing Lennox. "Ye had better ready yerself and yer men, Mackay," he ordered, his voice flat now. "For *ye* shall be escorting my daughter to Iona."

2: OUTSIDERS

DAVINA WAS SHAKING by the time she reached her bedchamber.

Closing the door behind her, she leaned against it, her heart pounding.

She'd tried to convince her father to permit this for months now—had asked her father at every opportunity to let her take the vow at Iona. He'd denied her every time.

But tonight, his patience had snapped.

Raising a hand to her still-stinging cheek, Davina closed her eyes.

Da had never hit her before, even in the blackest of rages. Yet things had gone too far. They'd both uttered words that could never be taken back.

Indeed, the things he'd said to her had hurt worse than that slap.

And her victory, as heady as it was, had left a bitter taste in her mouth.

Ye will be dead to me. Those words had turned her cold, as had the tone he'd used to deliver them.

Her father meant it.

Once she rode away from Kilchurn Castle, from him, there would be no going back. "I'm sorry it has to be this way, Da," Davina whispered, pushing herself off the door and walking across the chamber.

With a heavy sigh, she knelt on the wooden floorboards and reached out to withdraw two leather satchels from under the bed. She'd try to pack lightly, for she wouldn't be allowed to bring much with her into the abbey.

Davina drew the satchels out carefully, wary of dislodging any spiders from under the bed.

She *detested* spiders.

Placing the bags down next to her, she knelt before a large wooden trunk that sat against the wall. She then threw it open and started pulling out the clothing she'd need for the journey.

This situation seemed surreal; she couldn't believe she was leaving. She went through the motions of packing, yet her mind was elsewhere. Now that she'd gotten what she desired, the fight had gone out of her. Her insides felt hollow. And as the moments stretched out, a discomforting blend of melancholy, regret, and resignation rushed in to fill the void.

This castle, around two years old now, held bittersweet memories.

When she'd first moved here, and had viewed the lofty curtain walls and tower house reflecting against the mirrored surface of Loch Awe for the first time, her heart had soared. She'd reined in her garron, glancing right at the handsome man riding next to her, and they'd shared a smile.

Captain Blair Cameron.

Davina halted in her packing, a kirtle in each hand, her eyes fluttering closed once more.

A year had passed since his death, yet nausea still stung the back of her throat, and grief twisted under her ribcage, when she remembered his knife-fight with her father.

Davina squeezed her eyes shut, attempting to banish the painful memories.

She didn't want to think of violence, blood, and death whenever she recalled her lover. Instead, she wanted to remember Blair's boyish smile, the cleft in his chin, and the way his moss-green eyes crinkled at the corners when he laughed.

Blinking as tears stung the back of her eyelids, Davina folded up the two kirtles and placed them in one of the satchels. Shortly, her maid, Kenna, would hear of what had transpired. The lass would come up and insist on helping her pack—but for the moment, Davina was glad of the solitude.

No, this fortress held too many reminders, both good and bad. Initially, coming to live here had been exciting, as love flowered between her and Blair, but these days, it felt like an ill-fitting shoe. Kilchurn chafed at her daily. With her lover dead, she was an outsider here.

Iona Abbey would offer her the escape she craved. Of course, her father was right—she'd never been overly pious, much to her late mother's disappointment, but after Blair's death, she'd thought much about her choices—her mistakes. In truth, she was too easily led by her reckless impulses. Her new life would be a chance to reinvent herself.

Lennox strode out into the castle bailey, cutting across to the guard barracks. It was a warm summer's eve, and the sun still hadn't set. Instead, the sky above was awash with ribbons of lilac, red, and gold.

Aye, it was a bonnie sunset, yet Lennox ignored it. Instead, a frown creased his brow.

He didn't have the time to play escort to the laird's willful daughter.

He was busy here. He'd just recruited five new guards—all of whom were incredibly green and in desperate need of training.

Lennox huffed out an irritated breath. *Don't fash yerself, man. Taking Campbell's daughter to the nunnery is an easy enough task.*

It wouldn't be an overly arduous journey, for it would only take them around three days to ride to the port of Oban. From there, they'd find a birlinn that would transport them to Iona—the tiny isle just off the western coast of Mull. If the weather held and the seas were calm, he could be back here within eight days.

Entering the barrack's common room, Lennox halted, his gaze sweeping over the men inside.

A watch of eight guards stood atop the walls, yet the rest of them were enjoying tankards of ale, looking on as a group of four men played knucklebones. Laughter and the rumble of male conversation halted at the sight of their captain. Unsmiling faces turned to him.

Lennox swept his gaze over his men. He pretended to ignore their cool welcome, yet his spine stiffened. They were all proud Campbells, and although they had no quarrel with the Mackays, one or two of them had challenged Lennox's authority over the past months.

Their former captain, the one Colin Campbell had slain, hadn't been a clansman either. Yet it seemed that the guards respected Blair Cameron greatly—and Lennox was a poor substitute. He'd been forced to prove himself, and he had. His years working as bailiff had given him a tough, inflexible edge. He'd now established his position here. Aye, some of these warriors still didn't like him much, but he didn't care.

He wasn't their friend but their captain.

Lennox caught the glint in the men's eyes then. Of course, most of them had been eating their supper in the hall earlier and had witnessed the altercation between Campbell and his daughter. The news would have already raced through the castle; there was no point in Lennox announcing it.

"Good eve, lads," he greeted them gruffly. "I need five of ye to join me tomorrow."

Silence followed this announcement.

Lennox's gut tensed as the moments slid by. He'd hoped for volunteers, but none were forthcoming. All the same, he was careful not to let his irritation show.

"Hamish." His gaze settled upon a big, rawboned man with a receding hairline. "Ye are coming with me."

The warrior nodded, his mouth compressing slightly.

Lennox's gaze shifted to the guards who'd been playing knucklebones. "As are ye ... Keith, Archie,

Fergus, and Elliot." He paused then, his gaze narrowing. "Make sure ye're all ready before dawn tomorrow."

A chorus of terse 'ayes' followed—and then Lennox turned on his heel and left the barracks. There was little point in lingering; his presence wasn't welcome.

He'd intended to return to the tower house after informing his men of their departure, but instead, his feet carried him to the stone steps leading up to the walls.

Some of his old restlessness plagued him these days—a sensation he'd thought he'd left behind when he took up this position. He should return to his bedchamber and pack a few things for the morning, but that could wait.

Climbing the steps, Lennox alighted upon the wall, nodding to the sentry posted to his right.

This wall looked south, across Loch Awe. The sun had almost finished setting now. The spectacular sunset had faded to a rosy glow to the west, while the rest of the sky had turned a deep indigo. A few stars had twinkled into view, and the shell of the moon was rising.

It was a fine view—breathtaking even—yet Lennox was too irritated this evening to enjoy it.

Irritated that Campbell was treating him like his errand boy.

That even after five months, he was still an outsider here.

And that throwing in his position as bailiff of his brother's lands on the Kintyre peninsula and taking this new role hadn't brought him the satisfaction he'd hoped for.

Lennox had always been restless. Even as a lad, he'd been the one who'd got himself, and his brothers, into trouble. The one who'd start a scrap. The one who'd push things to the limit.

As the second-born son, he'd imagined he would be chosen to lead the Dun Ugadale Guard, but the laird—his brother, Iver—had chosen Kerr, their younger brother, for the position. Instead, Lennox had worked for years as Iver's bailiff—a role he'd grown to hate.

It had also made him an unpopular man upon the peninsula. Bairns would start wailing, and women would run inside their bothies to hide when the chieftain's bailiff rode in. His primary role had been to collect rents, but there were always debts to be paid and petty criminals to be hunted down and arrested.

And with the years, Lennox's resentment had festered and grown, souring his once healthy relationship with his elder brother.

Clenching his fists by his sides, Lennox approached the battlements that ringed the high curtain wall. He should have known that a man couldn't escape his demons just by changing location—and yet he'd dared to hope. He was the black sheep among his brothers. Even Brodie, the youngest, who had a dour temperament, felt more at home within the walls of Dun Ugadale than he had.

And yet he missed it.

Mouth thinning, he stopped at the gap between two battlements and gazed south over the gleaming surface of the loch. The dying light made the still waters look as if they were coated in oil.

With effort, he unclenched his hands, flexing his fingers to loosen the cramping muscles.

Aye, Kilchurn Castle was gleaming new and breathtakingly grand. But all the same, he longed for the bare hills of the Kintyre peninsula, the taste of salt in the air, and the moss and lichen-encrusted walls of his brother's broch outlined against the wild sky.

Sometimes, like now, he longed for it with a fierceness that made his chest ache.

It galled Lennox to admit it, but he didn't belong here. He wasn't a Campbell. He was a Mackay, and his soul ached to be amongst his own people once more.

Yet pride wouldn't let him give in to the desire.

The thought of telling Colin Campbell he'd have to find a new captain, and of having to return to Dun Ugadale and ask for his old position back, made his bowels cramp.

Heaviness pressed down upon him then, replacing the yearning for his birthplace, his clan—a gnawing sense of hopelessness.

No. He'd made his bed, and he would have to lie in it.

Brooding, Lennox stood there awhile, listening to the silence of the gathering dusk. A veil of peace settled over the world at this hour, the quiet so profound that he could hear the steady thud of his pulse in his ears.

Eventually though, he huffed a deep sigh. He couldn't stand out here brooding all night. He needed to pack and get some sleep, for they had an early start in the morning.

However, as he turned, his gaze slid to the left—and he caught sight of a slender figure standing at the eastern ramparts. It was a mild evening, and so Lady Davina was clad only in a dark-blue kirtle—one that matched the hue of the sky. Her long black hair, usually braided and wound around the crown of her head in an austere style, rippled down her straight back.

She was staring out across the loch, toward the mountains beyond, oblivious to anything else.

Lennox stilled, his brow furrowing.

It was rare to see Campbell's daughter on the walls. Despite that it was summer, and the weather had been warm and settled of late, she didn't even venture out for strolls along the loch shore. Instead, she spent most of her day locked away in her solar.

Lennox's mouth thinned. The air of quiet tragedy that surrounded the woman this eve annoyed him. She'd gotten what she wanted, hadn't she? Thanks to her, he and five of his men had to leave their posts and make the trip to Iona. She should be abed, ensuring she rested up before the journey, not drifting around the castle like a ghost.

Another, irritated, sigh escaped him.

Instead of taking the stairs back down to the bailey, Lennox approached the laird's daughter.

3: DEAD TO HIM

"LADY DAVINA."

A male voice intruded, jerking Davina from her introspection. Turning from the wall, her gaze alighted on the tall man, clad in leather braies and a padded gambeson, swaggering toward her.

And Lennox Mackay *did* swagger.

Everything about the man who'd replaced her beloved Blair as Captain of the Kilchurn Guard oozed arrogance. At mealtimes in the hall, he sprawled indolently in his seat. His voice, a low drawl, got on her nerves, as did his lazy smile, and she did her best to ignore him.

Even so, she'd noted Mackay was a loner. Apart from her father, he didn't appear to spend time with anyone else in the keep. Unlike Blair, she had never seen him laughing with his men. Indeed, like her, he was alone on the wall this evening.

As he drew near, she saw his brows were knitted together. At least he was sparing her his usual smug grin.

"Captain Mackay," she greeted him crisply.

He halted a few feet back, his gaze sweeping her face. "Is something amiss, my lady?"

She stiffened. "No ... why do ye ask?"

"It grows late, and we have an early start in the morning. I expected ye abed, not standing upon the walls."

Davina frowned. "*We* have an early start?" she queried.

He nodded, his mouth pursing. "Aye ... I'm to lead yer escort."

Davina glanced away, even if tension curled up within her. She wanted a man she trusted, like the castle steward, Athol MacNab, to head her escort. Not this conceited peacock. "I have readied my belongings for tomorrow," she said after a brief pause, deliberately not looking his way. "And fear not ... I shall be well-rested at dawn." She paused then, irritated that she was having to explain herself to him. "But since I will never see this castle, or this loch, again, I wished to say my farewells."

He didn't reply, and the silence between them drew out.

It wasn't a comfortable pause though, and Davina clenched her jaw. Couldn't he just walk off and let her be?

And yet he didn't. He merely waited there, as if he expected her to be the first to leave.

Eventually, she turned to face him once more.

Lennox Mackay had folded his arms over his chest and was watching her with a hooded gaze. Something in the way he looked at her made Davina's hackles rise. Ever since the altercation with her father, she'd felt exhausted, wrung out. And once she'd finished packing, a strange numbness had descended over her.

But this man's presence had pierced it.

"Did ye want anything, Captain?" she asked, her voice clipped.

"No." There was a cool edge to his tone now.

"Well, then ... I shall bid ye good eve."

He inclined his head. "Good eve, Lady Davina. Sleep well."

Nonetheless, he didn't move away as she'd hoped. The infuriating man just stood there. He was beneath her in rank, yet he was making it clear he was to be obeyed.

Anger sparked in her belly, warming the chill that had settled there as she'd packed. Why were men compelled to dominate women? It was as if they were scared a strong female might unman them in some way. God forbid, she might have a will of her own.

Davina ground her teeth together. She was heartily tired of being bossed around. Since Blair's death, her father had tried to bend her to his will. Her poor mother had been easy to sway, for she'd had a gentle temperament and been eager to please. But Davina wasn't like Aileen. Instead, she'd inherited her father's stubbornness.

And so, she faced Lennox Mackay and folded her arms over her chest, mirroring his gesture. "And ye too, Captain. Fear not, I shall retire shortly. However, for the moment, I wish for some solitude. If ye don't mind."

A muscle feathered in Mackay's jaw, and his reaction pleased her. He could bristle all he wanted. He served *her*, not the other way around. And if he was to lead her escort, Mackay needed to know his place. She wouldn't spend the journey being ordered around by him.

Her pulse quickened then. Soon, she'd be on Iona, within the refuge of the convent. There, no man would dictate to her ever again.

The realization made her feel a little light-headed.

It struck her then that this was the first real exchange she and Mackay had ever had. During his months at Kilchurn, they'd barely said more than a handful of words to each other. There had been no need.

The moment stretched out, and Davina tensed, readying herself to do battle.

But, to her surprise, he admitted defeat. Favoring her with a curt nod, Mackay turned on his heel and stalked off.

Davina watched him go, her mouth lifting a fraction at the corners.

He wasn't swaggering *now*.

Lennox descended the steps to the bailey, his pulse thumping in his ears.

Why had he let the chit get to him?

The imperious tilt of Davina's chin as she'd stared up at him, the clipped edge to her voice as she'd replied, had goaded him, piercing the heaviness that had shrouded him as he stood atop the wall.

He'd merely reminded her that it was late and that she should retire, yet her entire body had vibrated with annoyance at his intrusion. She'd then dismissed him as if he were a servant.

He was a chieftain's son, not some lackey.

Muttering a curse under his breath, Lennox cut across the bailey, where flickering torches hanging on chains illuminated the gloom.

Davina might have appeared a waif, yet he'd already seen she had a tongue sharp enough to rival his mother's. Her haughtiness, her cool dismissal, was galling.

Reaching the steps that led inside, Lennox's mouth thinned. He wasn't looking forward to traveling with Campbell's daughter.

Ignore the woman, he counseled himself. *Just a few days, and she'll be someone else's responsibility.*

Her father didn't come out to see her off.

Of course, Davina had been expecting as much, yet the laird's absence as she waited in the bailey for Captain Mackay and his men to ready their horses made an ache rise under her breastbone.

Her father had meant his words then.

She was now dead to him.

It wasn't a cold morning—the air was mild with the sweet smell of summer—but Davina shivered, nonetheless.

"Are ye cold, lass?" Athol MacNab's gravelly voice caught her attention then. The steward, a weathered man with a kindly face, had emerged from the tower house. His gaze was tinged with concern as it settled upon her.

Davina shook her head. She wore a fine woolen cloak about her shoulders; once the sun rose, she'd likely have to remove it.

"No, I'm well, thank ye, Athol."

The steward approached her. And then, to her surprise, he reached out and took her hands, squeezing them gently. His grip was warm and strong, reassuring, although the gesture caught Davina unawares, and her throat thickened, tears pricking at the back of her eyes.

God's bones, she didn't want to weep.

Not after how hard she'd fought to leave this place.

But Athol, whom she'd known all her life, was looking at her with kindly concern, sadness tinging his eyes.

"I shall miss ye, Davina," he murmured, his voice roughening. "And so will yer Da."

Davina gave a soft snort. "I think not," she whispered. "He will be happy to be rid of me."

Their gazes met and held a moment before the steward shook his head. "Colin does a fine job of pretending otherwise these days, but he still adores ye, lass."

Davina swallowed as her throat tightened further.

Athol was kind, yet she doubted his words. These days, all her father wanted was for her to obey him. When she'd fallen in love with a man who didn't have lands or a title Campbell could benefit from, he'd taken him from her.

The reminder made resolve square her shoulders and tighten her stomach.

No, the steward meant well, but he was wrong; his loyalty to her father blinded him. The man she'd once adored was lost to her.

The rasp of a cleared throat behind her made Davina glance over her shoulder. Captain Mackay stood there, holding her palfrey by the reins. "Are ye ready, Lady Davina?"

She nodded before turning back to the steward. Squeezing his hands gently, she extricated her own from his grip. "All the best, Athol," she murmured. "I shall keep ye in my prayers, always."

And once she arrived at Iona, she'd have plenty of time to dedicate herself to prayer, to make up for the years when she'd focused on other matters.

MacNab bowed his head and stepped back from her. His eyes glittered with emotion.

Davina swallowed once more. Heaven help her, she needed to get away. Goodbyes were awful. She'd feel better once she was far from Kilchurn.

"Don't worry, Athol ... we'll make sure the lass gets to Iona safely," Hamish Campbell's gruff voice intruded then. Davina glanced over at where the older warrior stood next to his horse watching them. Hamish shared a look with her father's steward before meeting Davina's eye. His mouth then curved into a rare smile.

And despite the stone in her belly, Davina managed a wan smile in return. She'd known Hamish all her life. The warrior could be dour, yet he was warm-hearted and loyal; she was glad he was accompanying her on this journey.

Turning, she moved over to her palfrey. Thistle was a dainty grey mare her father had bought for her nearly a decade earlier. She was gentle and now nuzzled Davina's arm.

Davina's chest constricted. She was surprised the horse remembered her at all, for it was a long while since she'd gone riding. She rarely ventured out to the stables these days either.

But Thistle gave a soft whicker in greeting.

Davina's vision blurred.

"Here, Lady Davina," Captain Mackay said tersely. "I shall help ye up."

He cupped his hands then, allowing her to put her booted foot in them. An instant later, she vaulted lightly up onto the saddle. Blinking, in an effort to push back the tears, Davina concentrated on adjusting her skirts and slipping her feet into the stirrups.

"Do ye have the dowry?" MacNab asked the captain then.

"Aye," Mackay grunted. He seemed ill-tempered this morning. Clearly, he wasn't pleased about being charged with escorting her to Iona.

The clip-clop of shod hooves made Davina glance up, and she saw that a stable hand had led a stocky garron out of the stables. Two large leather bags had been strapped onto the pony's broad back: coins that would buy her entry into Iona.

Davina's pulse sped up; she imagined her father's thunderous face as he parted with those pennies. He'd always planned to give her husband a dowry, but this gift to the church would gall him. Her union with Ewan Stewart would have compensated him greatly in other ways and would have eased the sting of having to part with so much coin. But handing his daughter over to the church gave him nothing he valued.

"Guard it carefully," the steward warned, meeting Mackay's eye. "There's a king's ransom in there." Athol paused then, his brow furrowing. "With all the trouble between the crown and the Douglases, the roads aren't as safe as before ... last week, we had word of brigands on the highways."

The captain nodded, even as his mouth compressed. "Fear not, I shall protect both the *dowry* and Lady Davina." Mackay moved over to where his courser waited and swung up onto the saddle. Then, gathering the reins, he glanced around him at where the five other warriors who'd accompany them to Iona waited. They were viewing him with scowls and furrowed brows. "We ride out," he barked.

4: DON'T LOOK BACK

DAVINA DIDN'T GLANCE over her shoulder as they rode away from Kilchurn.

Even so, she felt the oppressive weight of the fortress at her back. It was almost as if she could sense someone's gaze upon her. Had her father gone up to the walls to watch her depart after all?

The urge to turn in the saddle, to see if he was there, was almost overwhelming—yet Davina fought it.

Nonetheless, it took all her will.

Shoulders hunching, hands gripping for grim death onto the reins, she kept her attention focused forward.

Before them, a salmon-colored sunrise flared across the eastern sky. Yet they weren't traveling in that direction.

Davina had been to Oban before and knew it wasn't an arduous trip. Initially, they would be taking the road west for a short while, before turning south and hugging the shore of Loch Awe as they rode southwest. The loch was a long one, and it made their journey circuitous, for they had to follow its course before striking north once they reached the coast. There would be two nights on the road to Oban, and then one more at the port itself before they set sail for Iona.

Keeping focused on the journey helped ease the crushing ache in her chest. Her father was oppressive, yet he was all she had. And despite everything, she loved him.

She had fine memories too, of the years before her mother sickened and died. He'd been softer then and had smiled more readily. She remembered how he'd bounced her on his knee when she'd been a lass, how he'd taught her to ride her first pony. He'd given her a puppy too—a Highland collie who'd been her faithful companion through the years of her childhood. Aye, he'd indulged her over the years, until he discovered her affair with his captain.

However, it hurt to cling to those memories, to remember the man he'd once been. Her protector. Her champion.

The past couple of years had changed Colin Campbell, just as they had her.

Once they cleared the causeway, the party of seven urged their horses forward into a brisk trot.

Davina rode behind Captain Mackay and two of his men, while the rest of the party—one of them leading the coin-laden garron—brought up the rear. The thunder of their horses' hooves echoed in the still morning across the glassy surface of the loch and off the sides of the mountains that cradled it.

It was an achingly beautiful morning, the kind that painters attempted to immortalize, but its glory merely caused unhappiness to twist harder still within Davina.

Goose, she chided herself. *This is what ye wanted, wasn't it?*

And it was. Blair's death had torn something asunder within her, something only starting afresh could heal.

Her father had also learned that his act of violence, of murder, had consequences.

He hadn't been sorry for what he'd done, but Davina wondered if he was so sure of himself now.

A heavy sigh gusted out of her then, even as she straightened her back and focused on Captain Mackay's broad shoulders up ahead. Indeed, it was best if she didn't take in her surroundings, or glance over her shoulder one last time at Kilchurn Castle.

Don't look back, lass.

It was time to face the future and leave the past behind her.

Shifting in the saddle, Lennox turned his gaze upon the party following him. They'd ridden at a steady pace all morning. He'd have preferred to ride faster, but with the garron and a lady companion, he kept to a brisk trot or sedate canter.

His gaze rested upon Lady Davina then, and he briefly met her gaze for the first time since leaving Kilchurn. "We'll stop for a short spell now," he announced. His tone was brusque, yet he couldn't help it. He'd awoken in a sour mood at dawn, and the journey so far hadn't sweetened his temper.

She favored him with a cool nod in response. Davina sat easily upon her grey palfrey. In the months he'd lived at Kilchurn, he hadn't seen her go out riding once. Instead, the stable hands had exercised Thistle.

Yet viewing her now, the woman looked as if she'd been born in the saddle. The fresh air and sunlight had already done her good too, for her usually wan cheeks had developed a slight bloom to them, and her brow glowed with sweat. She'd braided her hair down her back for the journey, although black strands had come free and now curled prettily around her face.

Prettily?

Lennox fought a frown. The woman was haughty and difficult. Surely, he didn't find her comely?

The party drew up their horses, loosening the beasts' girths and watering them at the loch's edge.

Lennox's men, after a few polite words to Lady Davina, moved away from their captain. Turning their backs on him, they sat down upon the shore to eat the noon meal the cooks had given them. They then started to talk amongst themselves, deliberately keeping their voices low, as if they didn't want their captain overhearing their conversation.

Farther up the shore, Lennox's mouth twisted. Their efforts were wasted. He didn't care what they gossiped about. He started on his own meal then. It was simple fare—fresh bread, butter, and boiled eggs, washed down with ale—but it was delicious.

Despite the cold-shoulder from his men, he ate heartily, although he noted that Davina nibbled at her meal like a mouse. It didn't surprise him. He didn't think he'd ever seen the woman eat with hunger or enjoyment. It was as if she ate merely to keep alive.

His jaw tightened. It annoyed him that she kept drawing his gaze, yet there was something about Campbell's daughter that made him want to look her way.

Seated upon a log at the water's edge, Davina appeared to have withdrawn into her own world. Her gaze remained on the mirrored surface of the loch while she ate. It was as if she had forgotten she had company. Sadness suffused her delicate features.

And despite himself—something within Lennox stilled at the sight.

He wondered if her sorrow was for her dead lover, or the father she was now estranged from.

The lass had been through much over the past year.

Of course, she'd behaved recklessly, and had given her heart—and her body too, if the rumors were true—to a man her father would never have let her marry.

Her situation reminded Lennox of his elder brother's hasty, and inappropriate, marriage.

When it came to women, Iver had once been too open-hearted and trusting. When he was younger, his brother had wooed lasses with earnest dedication, only to have his heart broken—twice. Iver had sworn off marriage and love, and for a while, Lennox had believed he'd never take a wife. But then, in February that year, when they'd visited Stirling for a king's council, Iver had lost his heart to a chambermaid named Bonnie—and he was now married to her.

Lennox had been perplexed at his brother's choice at the time and still didn't understand it. Aye, Bonnie was comely and sweet-natured, yet she was lowborn and illegitimate. He wondered then how things were going at Dun Ugadale for the couple. His mother wouldn't have made Bonnie's arrival easy. Was Iver still as besotted as he'd been months earlier?

Lennox couldn't help but feel a little scorn for his brother for losing his wits over a lass so. He'd made a fool of himself too, but he didn't seem to care. Lennox would never put himself in such a position.

A few yards distant, Davina blinked, coming out of her reverie. And, as if she felt the weight of his gaze, she looked Lennox's way.

He jolted, heat flushing over him at the realization she'd caught him staring. Embarrassed, he was tempted to look away, yet he fought the urge. If he did that, she'd get the upper hand—like she had the eve before.

And so, their gazes fused, their stare drawing out. The moments slid by, and neither of them broke it.

Lennox's senses sharpened, and an odd awareness tingled through his body. She was a bold one, indeed. No wonder she locked horns with her father so violently.

Davina's chin lifted a fraction then, her eyes narrowing.

Continuing to hold her eye, Lennox rose to the challenge. Two could play this game. Moments passed, and then he couldn't help but offer her a slow, goading smile.

Davina yanked her gaze away.

Curse him, he'd bested her.

She'd been finishing her meal, lost in her thoughts, when she'd sensed someone was watching her. And then her gaze had met Lennox Mackay's.

He'd been caught staring, yet the cur didn't even have the manners to look away, chagrined. No, instead, he'd continued to watch her with his usual brash self-confidence.

And as their stare drew out, Davina noted the color of his eyes for the first time: dark-blue, the hue of the sky just after dusk. Even though he'd lived at Kilchurn a few months, she hadn't noticed this detail before. Tall and long-limbed, Mackay had dark-blond hair that was cut short and had a mussed look, as if he'd just run his hands through it. He had a strong jaw, a straight nose, and high cheekbones. Aye, the man was roguishly attractive, and he likely knew it.

And then, when Davina frowned at him, the knave had smiled.

His sullen demeanor earlier that morning hadn't lasted long; his arrogance was back. Something about that smirk needled her. She couldn't hold his gaze after that—and now he'd won.

"Come on, lads." Mackay's voice echoed along the shoreline, all business now. "Time to move on. Let's ready the horses."

The warriors obeyed, although when Davina glanced in their direction, she saw that they did so grudgingly. Hamish wore a deep scowl, while Fergus muttered something under his breath, causing the warrior next to him, Archie, to give a derisive snort.

Davina inclined her head then. Aye, it was as she'd suspected. Lennox Mackay hadn't been fully accepted by his men. He'd sat apart from the others while they'd rested and had barely shared more than a handful of words with any of his warriors all morning. There wasn't any camaraderie between them—instead, she picked up on a simmering resentment. They minded Mackay, yet they didn't *like* him.

Of course, they'd looked up to Blair, and she wondered now if any of them resented her father over his death. None of them would dare openly criticize their laird—but they didn't have to accept the man Campbell had hired to replace Blair.

5: THE NIGHT OF THE SPIDER

SLIDING OFF THISTLE'S back, Davina winced.

Mother Mary, she was unused to riding. After a day in the saddle, the muscles in her backside and thighs were burning. She'd be stiff in the morning.

She then turned to her palfrey and stroked the mare's sweaty neck. "I've neglected ye, haven't I, lass?" she murmured. "And soon we shall part ways for good."

Thistle gave a soft snort and nudged at Davina's arm.

"Horses always appreciate being spoken to." A man's voice, laced with amusement, intruded, and Davina glanced up to see Captain Mackay standing next to his gelding a few yards away. "Many folk don't realize that."

Davina gave a stiff nod before turning back to her palfrey and starting to unsaddle it. "Aye, my father always told me to talk to my horse like it's a friend." Unfastening the saddle's girth, she then reached up once more, her hand sliding across the mare's shoulder. "Thistle has been with me for a long while."

"And yet ye never ride her."

Davina's mouth thinned. She didn't look Mackay's way as she grabbed hold of the saddle and hauled it off Thistle's back. "I've not been in the mood," she replied, so quietly she was sure he wouldn't hear her. However, when she turned with the saddle, she found the captain standing right in front of her.

"Here … let me take that," he said smoothly, flashing her a grin.

Davina frowned. She didn't trust his sudden chivalry. And she wished he'd wipe that annoying smirk off his face.

"I can do it," she replied. Indeed, her father had always insisted she unsaddle her horse and rub it down after a ride, for it showed the beast respect and helped bind the horse and its owner. Ironically, she often thought her father had a greater love for his horses and dogs than he did for his own daughter; he'd certainly shown them more tenderness than he had her, of late.

"I'm sure ye can." Mackay stepped forward and took the saddle from her, swinging it with ease over the high wooden partition that divided the stalls inside the stables. "But it's been a long day … and ye are tired."

Davina clenched her jaw. "What, ye have manners now, do ye?"

Mackay glanced her way, his smile fading. "Somehow, we seem to have gotten off on the wrong foot, my lady," he said, his tone sobering. "Maybe I wish to remedy that." Davina frowned, yet he continued, "I'll have one of the lads rub yer horse down. Go inside … I've spoken to the innkeeper, and he's preparing a chamber for ye as we speak."

"What do ye want us to do with the coin, my lady?" Hamish called out then from the stall opposite. The older warrior was seeing to the garron. The stocky pony was greedily snatching at hay from a feeder while Hamish unstrapped the heavy leather bags containing Davina's dowry.

Noting Mackay's frown, for the warrior should have asked *him* that question, Davina replied, "Carry them up to my chamber, thank ye, Hamish."

"Do ye think that's wise, Lady Davina?" Mackay asked stiffly. "That's a lot of coin to protect overnight."

Davina raised her chin, holding his gaze. "All the more reason for me to keep it close," she pointed out. "I can't risk losing that dowry … and *I* wish to take responsibility for it."

"The innkeeper assures me all the chambers have locks on the door, Captain," Hamish rumbled.

"Good," Mackay replied. "Even so, make sure my chamber is next to Lady Davina's." He nodded to Davina before gesturing once more toward the stable doors. "Go on, my lady. The rest of us will follow soon enough."

Davina went, although not without stroking Thistle's nose first. She then walked from the stables and stepped out into the gathering dusk.

It had been a glorious day—with warm, soft air and golden light that made the world beautiful. The sunset was just as lovely, and the western sky blazed as if on fire. They'd reached Eredine at the end of the day's travel, a small hamlet set amongst thick forest near the shore of Loch Awe. It was a bonnie spot, yet they wouldn't be lingering.

Heaving a sigh, and giving her aching backside a gentle rub, Davina crossed the empty stable yard to where the inn, a squat stone building with two wings behind it, crouched. The thick press of trees surrounded them, and the sharp scent of pine hung heavily in the air.

Inside the inn's common room, Davina found a scattering of local men seated at trestle tables. They looked up with interest when she entered. Ignoring them, Davina took a seat near the open doors, where a pleasant breeze wafted into the stuffy space, mingling with the toothsome aroma of baking pastry. The innkeeper's wife bustled over with a jug of ale and some cups. "Yer chamber will be ready presently, my lady," she assured her with a warm smile.

"Thank ye," Davina replied, smiling back. It felt strange to smile; the expression pulled at muscles in her face she hadn't used in a while.

"We have grouse pie for supper this eve … I hope that's pleasing to ye?'"

"Aye, that'll do nicely."

The innkeeper's wife bustled back to the kitchen, leaving Davina alone. It was pleasant sitting here quietly, and she was halfway through her cup of ale when the rest of her party entered the common room. Hamish and

Archie carried the coin-laden sacks and Davina's belongings upstairs to her chamber, while the others took a seat at a nearby table.

Lennox Mackay didn't join them. Instead, he sat down at her table. Reaching forward, he picked up the jug, pouring himself a cup of ale. Then, taking an experimental sip, he nodded. "Not bad."

Davina didn't answer. She wished he'd take the hint and move to another table. She was enjoying her own company and had been looking forward to dining on grouse pie—alone. But Mackay didn't move.

The remainder of their party descended the rickety wooden stairs then, and Hamish handed Davina a heavy iron key. "Yer things are all safely locked up in yer chamber, Lady Davina," he informed her.

Davina's mouth lifted at the corners. "Thank ye, Hamish."

The older warrior held her eye. "How are ye faring after the day's journey?"

"Well enough," she replied with a sigh. "Although I imagine I will feel it tomorrow."

"A hot bath should help remedy that, my lady," one of the other warriors, Fergus, called out. "Shall I ask for one to be brought up after supper?"

Her smile widened. "Aye, thank ye."

Davina turned back to her table, as Hamish joined the others, noticing that a groove had formed between Mackay's brows. Of course, he didn't have the easy familiarity that she did with her father's men-at-arms.

There was no warmth on their faces when they looked *his* way.

The innkeeper's wife and three serving lasses emerged from the kitchen then, bearing trays of fragrant pie. The men welcomed them with grins and words of praise as the women set the pies down in front of them. And despite the warning that they were still piping hot from the oven, they fell upon their supper like wolves.

Davina ate with more caution. Nonetheless, she had to admit the pie was delicious, with a suet pastry and well-seasoned filling. As she ate, she almost forgot

Lennox Mackay was seated just across the narrow circular table.

Unfortunately, the reprieve didn't last.

"The pie must be good," her table companion commented eventually. "I swear that's the first time I've seen ye eat with any enthusiasm."

Davina glanced up to see that the captain was watching her. His observation unnerved her a little. She hadn't realized he'd taken note of such things over the past months. Whenever they'd eaten in the hall at Kilchurn together, he'd appeared to ignore her.

In truth, she *was* a little hungry. The discovery surprised her. For a while now, her appetite had been poor. Melancholia had dogged her steps ever since Blair's death and robbed her enjoyment of food. "It must be all the sunlight and fresh air," she replied.

"I hear a nun's meals are sparse indeed." His mouth curved. "Bread and ale to break yer fast in the mornings, with little more than vegetable pottage and cheese at noon." He glanced down at the pie he'd nearly finished. "Ye certainly won't be getting fare like this."

Davina shrugged. "As long as they don't starve me, I care not."

A woman's shrill scream ripped Lennox from a deep slumber.

Catapulting himself from his bed, he staggered and put a hand out to steady himself against the lime-washed wall. Blinking, he tried to focus.

God's blood, what was that?

Another shriek traveled through the wall, and Lennox lunged for his braies.

Davina.

Rushing barefoot and half-naked from his chamber to the one next door, Lennox moved to the door and tried the handle. It was locked.

"Lady Davina!" he called. "Is something wrong?"

The patter of bare feet on wooden floorboards followed, and then the grate of a key in the lock.

An instant later, the door was yanked open, and Davina Campbell stood before him.

Lennox stilled at the sight of her.

Clad in nothing but a thin night-rail, her hair unbound, Davina seemed a different woman to the one he'd accompanied from Kilchurn. The night-rail was made of a thin gauzy material, and the glow of the lantern behind her outlined her lithe, naked form underneath.

Catching himself, Lennox snapped his gaze to her alarmed face. "What is it?"

"A spider," she gasped, her chest heaving with alarm. "It's huge!"

Lennox huffed out an annoyed sigh. "A spider? God's troth, woman. Ye screamed as if the Bean-Nighe herself had climbed in yer window."

Face flushed, gaze wide, Davina was too panicked to take offense at his tone. Instead, she shook her head and gestured frantically over her shoulder. "Look!"

Humoring her, even as his irritation quickened, Lennox's gaze traveled to the wall above her bed.

He frowned. The lass wasn't wrong. It was a beast. All the same, there hadn't been any need to scream the inn down. He wouldn't be surprised if she'd woken everyone. Fortunately, he couldn't hear any slamming doors or hurried footsteps behind him.

Entering the chamber, Lennox approached the wall, studying the insect. Covered in bristly brown hair, it had dark markings on its back and legs. "It's a wolf spider," he said after a moment. "Harmless enough."

"I can't sleep with it hanging over my head," she gasped. "What if it falls upon my face?"

"It's not likely to ... wolf spiders are shy. It's probably more afraid of ye than ye are of it."

Davina shuddered in response, wrapping her arms around her body. Indeed, she did look alarmed. "I don't like spiders," she admitted huskily. "Ever since my cousin tormented me with them as a bairn."

Lennox sensed her embarrassment then, which kindled like a flame now that her panic was subsiding. It was tempting to tease her, yet something prevented him. He needed to stop engaging with this woman so much. Soon enough, she'd be out of his life for good.

"I hope someone gave yer cousin a thrashing for such behavior," he replied.

She pursed her lips and then shook her head.

Loosing another sigh, Lennox raised an eyebrow. "Would ye like me to turf the spider out?"

She nodded. "Please."

"Right, raise the sacking on the window while I find something to pick it up with."

Davina moved to do as bid, while Lennox fetched an empty cup and the shovel from by the cold hearth. It wasn't a cool evening and so the innkeeper hadn't lit a fire. Moving across to the insect, he deftly placed the cup over it while scooping the shovel carefully up underneath. A moment later, he deposited the wolf spider out the window.

"Thank ye." Davina approached and lowered the sacking. "I appreciate yer assistance."

Her voice was low, and she appeared to be avoiding his gaze as she retrieved the cup and shovel from him and returned them to their former places.

"And I'm happy to be of assistance, Lady Davina," he replied. He couldn't help but let a teasing edge creep into his voice now.

Davina turned to him then, yet she didn't look at his face. Instead, her gaze rested on his bare chest. She'd done so to avoid his eye, yet as the moments drew out, he marked the way her lips parted ever so slightly, and how her gaze slowly slid down his torso to where the braies he'd hastily donned sat low on his hips.

Lennox went still. He couldn't believe it. The lady was *admiring* him.

And as the silence between them swelled, Lennox found himself paying her the same compliment.

Through her filmy night-rail, he could see the dark circles of her nipples and areole. Her breasts were small and pointed, and Lennox couldn't help it; he stared at them for a few moments before his gaze slid south, over her lissome form to the dark triangle of her sex.

His heart kicked against his breastbone then, and his groin stiffened.

Christ's blood, Davina Campbell wasn't the sort of woman he usually lusted after; he preferred his lasses buxom, with easy smiles and uncomplicated natures.

But, tonight, his body had other ideas.

6: WE ALL HAVE OUR WEAKNESSES

DAVINA'S PULSE STARTED thundering in her ears.

What in heaven's name are ye doing?

Initially, when Mackay had entered her bedchamber to aid her with the spider, she hadn't noticed the man was half-naked. She'd been too panicked to care about his state of dress.

But when she had, she'd stared like a lackwit.

To be honest, he was quite a sight. Lennox Mackay was leanly built, yet the lantern light gilded the hard muscles of his chest, shoulders, and arms. In this warm light, he appeared sculpted from marble.

She should have yanked her gaze away then, but instead, in a daze, she'd let her attention wander lower, to his flat belly and the waistband of his braies. He'd clearly pulled them on when he'd heard her screams, hastily knotting the laces. Yet the knot had now loosened, and the braies hung indecently low.

And as she stared, she saw movement in those loose trew.

With a jolt, she realized his rod was stiffening.

Mother Mary!

That was enough to jerk her out of the trance. Davina's head snapped up, hot mortification prickling across her skin.

He was staring at her, a blend of incredulity and heat in his gaze.

Davina's galloping heart went wild. He'd marked how blatantly she'd stared at him. Stumbling back, she gestured to the door. "Thank ye for yer assistance, Mackay." Her voice came out strangled, causing humiliation to pulse through her.

Ever since Blair, she'd told herself that no man would ever arouse her again. But to her dismay, desire was very much alive—for she'd just responded to someone she didn't even like.

And Mackay was looking at her now as if he wanted to devour her.

She had to get him out of her bedchamber before he tried anything.

"I was happy to help, my lady," he said, his voice low yet edged with faint amusement.

Davina's cheeks were burning now, and she clenched her hands by her sides. "Good night," she ground out. "Let us forget this happened."

Mackay moved toward Davina then, halting before her.

They were standing close, so close she could smell the woodsy scent of the soap he'd used to bathe with before retiring; mixed with the spicy aroma of his skin, the smell was heady.

Davina's breathing grew shallow, and an unwelcome ache started to pulse between her thighs.

Lord, did she have no shame?

"Davina," he rumbled softly. "Look at me."

Clenching her jaw, she slowly raised her chin and forced herself to meet his eye. Her heart thudded painfully against her ribs when she saw he was no longer amused. Instead, his expression smoldered.

This man had a breathtaking sensuality, one her body responded to like dry tinder to a flame. It was shocking to discover she didn't dislike him as much as she'd thought. Upsetting. It made Davina want to race outside and throw her heated body into the icy waters of Loch Awe to quench the fire.

"Are ye settled now that the spider has been dealt with?" he asked, his gaze never leaving hers.

"Aye," she whispered. What a lie that was. Her heart was pounding wildly. "I feel a little foolish now though."

His mouth quirked in a half-smile that made desire twist low in her stomach. "Don't feel embarrassed on my account," he murmured. Heat flushed across Davina's chest as she realized he wasn't only talking about the spider but about the awareness that had just sparked between them. "We all have our weaknesses."

And with that, he walked to the door and left the chamber, pulling the door shut behind him.

Standing alone in her bedchamber, Davina waited a few moments before breathing an oath. Curse it, she hadn't meant to shriek like a banshee either—but her fear of spiders had caused all good sense to flee. She then glanced down at where her breasts thrust against the thin material of her night-rail. Why hadn't she had the wits to don a robe before answering the door?

Although small, her breasts felt much heavier than usual, and her dark nipples were pressing against the thin linen as if the night were cold. But far worse was that the deep, uncomfortable ache between her thighs hadn't yet eased.

Shakily, Davina moved across to the bed.

Instead of retiring, she sank to her knees before it. The floorboards were hard, yet she welcomed the discomfort. Clasping her hands together, she squeezed her eyes closed. No, she wasn't devout—but she had to change that. Tonight. She couldn't enter Iona plagued by impure thoughts. "Our Father in Heaven," she whispered fervently. "Keep me from temptation ... from sin."

Davina bit her lower lip then, her chest constricting.

She hadn't cared about either of those things when she'd given in to her need for Blair Cameron. They should have waited until marriage to succumb to desire, yet during a warm, wet summer, they'd consummated months of lingering glances and stolen touches. But now Davina's lover was dead, and her days of reckless behavior were behind her.

"Just a few more days," she whispered, squeezing her hands together so hard her fingers started to hurt. "And I can start again."

Lennox brushed away a fly that kept diving at his face and glanced up at the hard blue sky.

Two hot days had passed since they'd left Kilchurn, and it looked as if today would be scorching as well. Usually, he welcomed good weather—for after months of grey and cold, it was a balm to feel the sun's warmth upon his skin—but he now found it stifling.

While they'd been riding alongside Loch Awe, the heat had been less oppressive. A faint breeze had feathered in across the water, fanning their sweaty brows and keeping the midges and flies away from the horses.

But now that they'd left the loch behind, it had grown increasingly humid.

At present, they rode through a thickly wooded vale, and clouds of midges, which had risen from the stream that ran alongside the road, were bothering the horses and riders alike.

Slowing his courser a little, Lennox allowed Davina to draw up alongside upon her palfrey. And to his chagrin, she looked much fresher and more comfortable than he did.

Arching an eyebrow, she favored him with a questioning look. "Is something amiss, Captain?" she asked, her tone as cool as her expression.

Lennox shook his head. In truth though, he was plagued by both boredom and irritation this morning. He had no real reason to feel so, for the journey had gone well so far. They'd stopped at the village of Kintraw on the second eve and found comfortable lodgings.

Yet, as he often did, Lennox had slept fitfully, and ever since leaving Kilchurn, he'd felt increasingly impatient.

He studied Davina's face a moment. After the incident with the spider at Eredine on the first night, they'd barely spoken; the woman had taken great pains to ignore him. The eve before at Kintraw, she'd disappeared into her room as soon as they found lodgings—and hadn't reappeared until this morning. She hadn't joined Lennox or his men for supper in the common room downstairs; instead, a serving lass brought her meal up to her.

Her cold shoulder shouldn't have bothered him yet, strangely, it had. He'd eaten his supper alone at a table in the common room, while his men diced and laughed a few yards away, and kept stealing glances at the stairs, as if expecting her to join them. It had dawned on him then, as he finished his meal, that he enjoyed sparring with Davina Campbell. The evening was dull without her.

"We have one last, long day of travel before us, Lady Davina," he replied with a smile. "I thought we might pass the time with some light conversation."

Her mouth compressed, letting him know she didn't find the idea appealing.

Indeed, part of Lennox knew he should leave well enough alone. The truth was, Davina had piqued his interest. He should heed her advice and forget that incident, and yet he couldn't. The night before, as he'd stared up at the darkness, he'd recalled the way she'd looked at him, and the way her small, peaked breasts thrust against her thin night-rail. He'd imagined going down on his knees before her and suckling those tempting nipples through the fine linen.

Letting himself indulge in such a fantasy had been a mistake though, for he'd had to deal with a raging erection.

Just get her to the gates of Iona Abbey, he'd told himself as he pressed his knuckles against his throbbing shaft. *And remember what Colin Campbell does to those who mess with his daughter.*

That warning should have been enough to make him keep his distance from Davina—and yet, over the past day, he'd fought the urge to seek her out, to have that haughty gaze upon him once more. And this morning, he'd given in to the temptation.

"I can't imagine what we'd talk about, Captain," Davina replied after a brief pause.

He inclined his head. "Do ye believe I lack the wits to engage ye in witty conversation then?"

A blush flared upon her cheeks, and her back stiffened. He'd thought she might deny it, yet to his surprise, she replied, "Perhaps."

Lennox barked a laugh. "I'm brother to the chieftain of Dun Ugadale, ye know?"

"Congratulations," she replied, her tone dry. Of course, she *would* know that, having met Iver a few months earlier.

"I was brought up with a tutor," Lennox went on. "I imagine I speak French and Latin just as well as ye do ... and I can discuss politics and philosophy too, if ye wish?"

Davina gave a soft snort. "Ye don't have to prove yerself to me, Captain. I care not for yer accomplishments."

Her words were meant to quash Lennox, yet he found they merely encouraged him. "Even so, ye have barely spoken since Eredine," he drawled. "I was beginning to think there was something wrong with yer tongue."

Stony silence met this comment. She likely didn't appreciate him mentioning that village, for it was a reminder of what had happened at the inn.

Flies buzzed around them, and their horses' tails swished, their ears flickering as they tried to dislodge the annoying insects. Judging from the baleful look Davina was giving him, Lennox guessed she wished she could flick him away like a fly.

He was aware that he was crossing a line, that he was starting to push a little too hard. Nonetheless, it was as if there were a devil on his shoulder this morning.

"I believe I have misjudged ye, Lennox Mackay," Davina said eventually, breaking the silence between them.

His mouth curved once more. "Ye did?" He thought he'd offended her, but maybe he hadn't, after all.

"Aye," she went on. "Ye come across as brash ... with the confidence of ten men ... but I believe that's a ruse. For all yer insolence, ye aren't as sure of yerself as ye make out."

Lennox's smile faded.

Like a well-aimed quarrel, Davina's observation had just hit him between the eyes. It was as if she'd just stripped away the mask he never took off, leaving him naked in front of her. And the feeling of exposure wasn't a sensation he liked—not at all.

He noted then that Davina was watching him closely, her gaze sharp. She knew she had him.

Lennox wasn't sure how he'd have responded then—although he never got the chance, for one of his men forestalled him. "Captain!" Hamish grunted from a few yards back. "Something is happening ahead."

Inwardly cursing himself for taking his attention from his surroundings, for he was usually vigilant, Lennox's gaze snapped forward.

They'd just rounded the corner. A moment earlier, their view of the road before them had been obscured by the low-hanging branches of oak trees. But now, he spied a skirmish only yards away. Three men were closing in on a fourth, their thin dirk-blades flashing in the sunlight.

7: MAKE YER CHOICE

CURSING, LENNOX HASTILY angled his courser in front of Davina's palfrey and pulled both horses up. As a precaution, he then drew his dirk.

"Who are they?" Davina asked, her voice tight with alarm.

"I don't know," Lennox replied, his gaze never leaving the fight. "None of the men are wearing clan plaid."

A curse echoed down the road, as the man they'd bailed up against a tree at the roadside—a big warrior with wild dark hair—sliced one of his assailants across the forearm with his dagger.

"I'll stick ye like a pig for that!" the injured man shouted.

"God's teeth," Davina whispered. Lennox had hoped to block her view of the fighting, yet she'd managed to peer around him. "They're going to kill him."

"Aye, that is likely," Lennox agreed.

Her eyes snapped wide. She then glanced back at where the rest of their party had drawn up their horses.

"We should keep out of this, Lady Davina." Archie spoke up, a warning in his voice. "This isn't our quarrel."

Lennox was inclined to agree with him. Nonetheless, things were looking grim for the dark-haired man. The bloodthirsty expressions on the three warriors who closed on him left Lennox in no doubt about what was about to happen.

Davina urged her palfrey closer to Lennox and reached out, her fingers closing around his forearm. "Can't ye stop them?" she gasped.

Something inside him jolted. Her hand was a brand on his skin.

"Mackay," Hamish barked. "We should leave them to it."

"We should," Lennox agreed, his gaze never leaving Davina's. It was good advice too. Every Highlander knew that no good ever came from getting involved in other people's fights.

Davina stared back at him, even as she removed her grasp on his arm. She didn't ask again, yet she didn't need to. The plea in those expressive grey-blue eyes said it all.

Moments passed, and then Lennox breathed a curse. God's blood, he couldn't believe he was doing this. He'd clearly left his wits behind him at Kilchurn.

An instant later, he angled his courser forward before calling out. "Halt!" The four men froze, their gazes snapping right to him. "That's enough, lads," Lennox greeted them. "Lower yer blades."

The warrior with the bleeding arm scowled at him. "And who are *ye* to issue orders?"

Meanwhile, the man the others had been attacking, whose back was now pressed up against the tree, remained silent. He was breathing hard, blood trickling down his cheek from a scratch beneath his eye.

"Just a traveler who wishes to prevent a lady from witnessing bloodshed," Lennox replied, his tone deliberately light, even as his grip tightened upon his dirk.

The men's gazes slid to where Davina sat astride her palfrey behind him, and then one of them sneered. Next to him, another warrior made a lewd gesture with his hips. This caused his companions to snort with laughter.

The injured warrior then spat on the ground. "Go on yer way, *fazart*, and let us conclude our business."

Lennox heaved a sigh. Now they'd called him a coward, he couldn't let things lie, could he? He slid his dirk back into its scabbard and instead reached for the longbow he carried strapped to the back of his saddle. He then withdrew an arrow from the quiver upon his back, and notched it.

"I believe ye didn't hear me the first time," he said, his tone still light. "But perhaps an arrow through the throat might make ye pay attention."

"Aye," a gruff voice accompanied Lennox's, and he realized that Hamish had ridden up alongside him. A quick glance in the warrior's direction confirmed that he too had readied his bow. The warrior's brow was furrowed as he stared down the three men standing just a handful of yards away. "I'm sure it would."

The injured man's expression sobered. He then glared at Lennox. "Stand back," he growled. "Ye are messing with things beyond yer ken."

"I think not," Lennox replied, drawing the bowstring just a little tighter. The arrow vibrated against his hand, screaming to be loosed.

"This man is a criminal," the man who'd made the lewd gesture added. His manner wasn't insolent now though. He looked worried. "Wanted by the *king*."

"That's a lie," the big man against the tree rasped. "I've done nothing wrong."

Lennox frowned. He was inclined to believe him rather than the others. They were a rough lot and didn't look like the king's emissaries. "Off ye all go," he murmured. "For my wrist tires ... I wouldn't want to accidentally shoot one of ye, would I?"

"Aye ... and go quietly," Hamish said, his tone threatening now. "Enough talk."

They went, although not without glowers and clenched jaws. One by one, each of the three warriors, still gripping their unsheathed dirks, moved back across the road and melted into the press of alders at the roadside.

Lennox watched them go, keeping the spot where they disappeared in his sights with his bow and arrow.

"Keith, Elliot, and Archie," he called out then. "Make sure our new friends are *really* on the run."

Wordlessly, the three warriors swung down from their horses, drew their dirks, and crashed through the undergrowth after the trio.

That left Lennox, Hamish, Fergus—and Davina—alone with the man they'd rescued.

Casting Davina a warning look, for he didn't want her getting close to the stranger, Lennox lowered his bow and arrow and urged his courser forward, approaching the man. And as he drew closer, recognition tickled at him. Lennox frowned. "Have we met before?"

The wild-haired individual stared back at him, his own brow furrowing. "I don't know," he admitted hoarsely. "Although ye do look familiar."

"My name's Lennox Mackay, Captain of the Kilchurn Guard ... and yers?"

The warrior nodded, his expression cautious. "And I am Brogan Douglas, cousin to the Earl of Douglas."

Lennox stilled—and then he remembered where he'd seen this man before.

Six months earlier in the stable yard at Stirling Castle.

There had been a group of angry Douglas warriors gathered there, surrounded by pike-wielding guards—and this man had been their leader. Brogan Douglas had swung down from the saddle, unpinned a scroll from his horse's tail, and thrust it into the hands of Stirling's seneschal. Letters of safe conduct.

Their clan-chief, murdered at the king's hands, had received such a letter—but it hadn't ensured William Douglas's safety. The clan had broken with the crown that day, and relations between the Douglases and the Stewarts had deteriorated ever since. William's younger brother, James, now led the clan. He'd openly denounced the king and taken up arms against him, thus making him an enemy.

Lennox's belly swooped.

Satan's cods, those men hadn't lied after all. This *was* king's business, and Lennox had interfered.

He started to sweat then. Thank the saints the warriors his own men were now chasing through the forest didn't know who he and his companions were. The last thing any of them needed was to bring the king's wrath down on their heads. Everyone knew that James was set on destroying the Douglases.

"Those men were Stewarts, weren't they?" Lennox asked after a tense silence.

Behind him, he heard Davina's stifled gasp.

Aye, she was right to be shocked. He should have left well alone, yet like a reckless idiot, he'd waded into the fight just to please her.

But it was done now.

Brogan's gaze was wary as he nodded. "They discovered I was traveling this way and intercepted me," he said roughly. His mouth twisted then. "The king shall not rest until every last Douglas is dead."

Lennox inwardly cursed.

"Aye, well, it's just as well we came upon ye when we did," Davina spoke up cautiously then. When Lennox glanced over his shoulder, he saw that her gaze was veiled. "Or they would have had ye."

"And I am forever in yer debt, my lady." Brogan Douglas sheathed his dirk and lowered himself onto one knee, bowing his head. "May I know the name of my avenging angel?"

Lennox scowled. Douglas looked a rough-mannered sort, yet he knew courtly language, it seemed. And he knew how to ingratiate himself too.

Davina merely favored the man with a tight smile. "I am Lady Davina Campbell," she replied. "Although yer thanks should go to Captain Mackay, not me."

Douglas glanced up, his dark gaze glinting. "The Lord of Glenorchy's daughter?"

"Aye, what of it?" Lennox replied before Davina could, his tone sharpening.

"They're running for the hills, Captain." Lennox turned to see his men had returned. Unlike earlier, Archie was grinning. "Cursing us all the while, they were."

"Good." Lennox's gaze swept his men's faces. "Mount up, we'd best be on our way."

In truth, he was itching to ride on. The faster they got away from here the better. Best they left this incident, and Brogan Douglas, far behind them.

But luck wasn't on his side today, it seemed, for Douglas rose to his feet, brushing dust off his braies, and addressed Davina once more. "Are ye heading to Oban?"

Silence followed this question. Lennox ground his teeth and was about to tell Douglas their destination was none of his business when Davina gave a slight, reluctant nod.

Douglas flashed her a toothy smile. "Well, that's a happy coincidence, my lady," he rumbled, "for so am I." His expression tightened then, his gaze shadowing. "I was planning to find a ship to one of the isles so that I might disappear for a while. As ye can see, I'm a hunted man here on the mainland."

"Why don't ye return to yer kin?" Lennox asked.

Douglas glanced his way, his heavy brow furrowing. "James has been forced to abandon Drumlanrig Castle ... he and his men are all in hiding at present. We were separated three months ago, and I've been searching for them ever since."

A heavy silence followed as Lennox's men swung up onto the back of their horses, before Douglas eventually shattered it. His gaze had returned to Davina. "I don't suppose one of yer escort would let me ride with him, my lady?" he asked. "I'm weary enough to drop."

Davina's mouth compressed, her slender shoulders tensing. She then glanced over at Lennox, meeting his eye. A long look passed between them. Once again, although she didn't speak a word, he read her silent request. The woman was entirely too soft-hearted, although it seemed so was he.

Lennox's gut clenched. God's teeth, Douglas was a wily bastard; he knew exactly how to get what he wanted. "Very well," Lennox ground out after a tense pause. He then gestured to where one of his men sat upon a heavyset gelding. "Keith will take ye."

Keith, a solid young man with straw-colored hair, frowned at this.

Brogan Douglas bowed his head in thanks to Lennox before meeting Davina's eye once more. "Yer kindness humbles me, my lady."

Lennox's patience snapped. "Enough blether," he growled. "Get yer arse up on that horse and let us be off … we've been delayed here long enough."

8: I DARE

THEY SET OFF briskly, cantering along the dirt road under the dappled shade of alder and hornbeam, the tattoo of their horses' hooves echoing through the shimmering heat of the late morning.

Riding directly behind Mackay, Davina tried to quash the uneasy sensation that had twisted her belly in knots.

I shouldn't have asked him to intercede. Aye, things had been about to get bloody, yet she'd been surprised when the captain stepped in to stop the fighting. She hadn't thought he'd heed her.

Afterward, upon learning the men they'd chased off were Stewarts, and the warrior whose life she'd saved was a wanted man, she'd started to feel a little queasy.

Da would be furious with us for helping him.

Indeed, Colin Campbell was doggedly loyal to King James the Second. He'd made his dislike of the Douglases clear too. 'Traitors to the crown', he called them.

Davina's heart started to thud against her breastbone.

Her gaze settled once more upon the tense line of Lennox Mackay's shoulders. No doubt, he regretted intervening. Like her, he'd be worried about the repercussions. Davina started to sweat then. God's blood, this journey was supposed to be an easy one, yet so far, it had been far from straightforward. Thank goodness they were only half a day's ride out from Oban now and would reach the port before dusk. After that, all that would remain was a boat ride to Iona.

Finally then, she couldn't cause any more trouble.

They picked up the pace, making up for lost time, before taking their noon meal later than planned. The road had left the woodland now and led across undulating hills. To the west, Davina could see the blue slash of the sea against the horizon.

Resting by the roadside, she found a stump to sit on while Thistle nipped at grass, and unwrapped a pork pie the cooks at the last inn had provided them with. She'd been looking forward to it, pleased that her appetite had improved. However, the incident earlier in the morning had put her on edge. It had destroyed *all* their peace. Mackay hadn't stopped frowning ever since, and his men had gone quiet.

Davina nibbled at her pie, watching Mackay's men talking quietly together amongst themselves a few yards off. As always, their captain stood apart, eating his noon meal with the horses.

Brogan Douglas also kept to himself. The man sat under an oak tree a few yards distant. Catching Davina's eye, he flashed her a smile, pushed himself up off the ground, and approached her. "It seems yer companions think I'm a leper," he rumbled, still smiling, "but would ye mind if I sat with ye, instead, my lady?"

His request was polite; it seemed churlish to refuse it. "Of course not," she murmured.

Douglas sat down. Unlike Davina and her escort, he didn't have anything to eat. Instead, he stared at the pork pie she was eating. His gaze was intent, like a starved dog eyeing a banquet. Davina noted that the scratch beneath his eye had crusted; fortunately for him, it appeared to be a shallow wound.

The moments stretched out, and eventually Davina couldn't bear it any longer. She withdrew another pie from the parcel on her lap and held it out to him. "Here … ye look like it's been a while since yer last decent meal."

The man reeked, and underneath his wild hair and unshaven chin, she noted that his cheeks were hollowed. Life as a hunted man wasn't easy.

Douglas flashed her a grateful smile and took the pie she offered. "My thanks ... once again."

Davina didn't reply, instead watching as he wolfed the pie down in just a few bites.

A few yards away, Lennox Mackay turned, his gaze narrowing when it settled on Davina and her companion. He then swallowed the last of his meal and headed toward the tree stump.

Meanwhile, Douglas brushed the crumbs off his filthy braies and glanced Davina's way. "What takes ye to Oban, my lady?"

Davina frowned. Brogan Douglas was far too inquisitive for her liking.

As if sensing her distrust, he flashed her a contrite smile. "Apologies, if ye find my questions intrusive, my lady," he rumbled. "But I'm only making conversation."

Davina's cheeks warmed. Now, he thought her rude.

"I will see if I can earn my passage to one of the isles from Oban," Douglas volunteered before his gaze shadowed. "It's a terrible thing ... to see yer clan persecuted ... hunted like vermin. I've had enough of it. I only want to find somewhere I can live in peace."

Davina took this in, pity stirring within her. She then sighed before answering, "I'm taking a birlinn to Iona from Oban."

His dark gaze widened. "Ye are taking the veil?"

"Aye."

Douglas inclined his head. His lips parted, as if to say something else, but Mackay's arrival forestalled him.

The captain's shadow fell over them. "We need to get going," he said curtly, his sharp gaze spearing the outlaw. "Douglas, ye are riding with Keith again."

A relieved smile tugged at Davina's lips when, eventually, Oban hove into sight. They'd been following the coast for a while, as the shadows lengthened—and there it was, a jumble of tall stone buildings pressed around a busy quay on the horse-shoe-shaped Firth of Lorne.

They rode along the seafront, past where fishing boats and birlinns bobbed on the tide, before Davina waited while Captain Mackay strode off to see about getting them passage to Iona the following morning.

Meanwhile, Brogan Douglas slid down from where he'd been riding behind Keith and stretched out his stiff back.

"What will ye do now?" Davina asked him. Now that they'd reached their destination and would part ways, she felt safe to ask him such a question.

He flashed her a tired smile. "I suppose I shall see about finding work on a boat," he replied, "so I can earn my passage."

"Well, ye'd better get moving," Hamish grunted. "For it grows late in the day."

Douglas huffed a deep sigh, his gaze never leaving Davina's face. "I don't suppose a weary traveler could call upon yer generosity once more, my lady?" he murmured. "I'd be forever grateful if ye would grant me lodgings for the night."

Davina tensed at the bold request, while Hamish muttered a curse under his breath. "Ye go too far, Douglas," he growled. "Now, why don't ye move off before I make ye."

The outlaw ignored him. Instead, he favored Davina with a beseeching look. "Please, Lady Davina. I've been hunted and persecuted for months now and don't deserve the price on my head. King James has a cruel temper and a hatred for my clan ... am I to be punished for that?"

Davina's breathing grew shallow. The man was making her feel like only a beast would refuse him. "No," she said softly.

"Just a bed for the night," he rasped. "That's all I ask."

The desperation in his dark eyes was almost unbearable to look upon, and Davina sighed before relenting. "Very well."

"Lady Davina," Hamish muttered under his breath. "I don't think—"

However, Davina cut the warrior a quelling look, and his complaint choked off.

"What the devil is wrong with ye?"

"Excuse me?"

"Ye heard me, Davina. It's bad enough that we stuck our noses into the conflict between the Stewarts and the Douglases earlier ... but befriending an outlaw is taking things too far."

Lady Davina stared back at Lennox, her gaze widening at his bluntness. "The man is desperate," she replied, her tone sharpening. "Ye are overreacting, Mackay. I'm only giving him a room for the night ... not my dowry."

Lennox scowled. He'd returned from finding a captain willing to take them to Iona the following morning, only to discover that Davina had agreed to pay for Douglas's meal and lodgings. The outlaw had even managed to wrangle a bath out of her.

Not wanting to create a scene in front of his men, who'd all worn sour expressions, Lennox waited until they'd found an inn on the seafront, and had stabled their horses, before cornering the lady he was escorting in the hallway outside her chamber.

"The man can't be trusted," Lennox ground out. He was being aggressive and half-expected her to shrink back against the door and lower her gaze. But he should have known better. That wasn't Davina's way.

No, instead, her slender jaw locked, and her finely-arched black eyebrows snapped together. "Brogan

Douglas is no danger to me ... or ye," she replied coldly. "I don't see what the problem is."

"The man has been named an enemy of the King of Scotland," Lennox shot back. "That means that by spending time with him ... and not turning him over to the local bailiff ... *we* are committing treason."

Her cheeks flushed. "That's ridiculous!"

"No, it's the truth."

Her throat bobbed, betraying her sudden nervousness. "But no one here knows who he is."

"And thank Christ for that." Lennox took a step closer to her. They were only a couple of feet apart now, and Davina had to tilt her chin upward to hold his gaze. Yet she did. "Yer father charged me with yer safety, my lady ... but ye don't make my task an easy one when ye let a scoundrel browbeat ye."

Her lips parted, an outraged gasp escaping.

And Lennox couldn't help it; his gaze traveled to her mouth. It was small yet lush, cherry-red, and bow-shaped. He wondered then if it would taste as sweet as it looked.

Satan's cods, man. Concentrate!

Lennox's attention snapped back to her angry gaze, his own temper spiking once more. That was better. He needed to keep focused.

"How dare ye speak to me thus?" she croaked, taking a step back. Her spine was now pressed up against the door; there wasn't anywhere to go but through it.

Without second-guessing himself, Lennox moved forward, following her. Suddenly, they were so close he could smell lilac and the sweet scent of her skin; he noted the flecks of grey and blue in her wide eyes. "I *dare*."

Their gazes fused, and it occurred to Lennox then that if anyone—his men or Douglas included—climbed the stairs right now to the second floor, where their party was lodged, they'd find the Captain of the Kilchurn Guard and Lady Campbell in what appeared to be a compromising position.

Lennox wasn't done arguing with her, yet he didn't want to compromise her either. As such, he reached out, his fingers curling around the door handle. Stepping closer still, so close their bodies almost brushed, he pushed the door open behind them.

Davina staggered back through it, and he followed her.

9: TEMPTATION

DAVINA'S BREATHING WAS coming in short, shallow pants as she moved into her bedchamber.

She intended to slam the door in Lennox Mackay's face, but he was too quick. In an instant, the man was inside the room with her, the door thudding shut behind him—sealing them inside together.

"Knave!" she gasped. "Get out!"

"I'll leave when I'm ready," he replied, biting out each word. The captain's handsome face was all taut angles now, his dark-blue eyes almost black. "But not before ye admit that ye should have asked me before inviting Brogan Douglas to reside under the same roof as us."

Davina's heart started kicking like a wild pony against her ribs.

"I don't answer to ye, Mackay," she spat, even as she edged away from him.

They were both vexed, yet his closeness had an unnerving effect on her. Through the crimson haze of her anger, she was aware of the heat and strength of his body. The smell of pine and leather had filled her nostrils moments earlier when he'd reached forward to open the door—and she'd found herself dragging it deep into her lungs.

Being alone with this man was a bad idea. Eredine had shown her that. But here he was, stalking toward her as she shuffled backward. And when the back of Davina's thighs hit the edge of the bed, dizziness swept over her. She was cornered again, and Mackay was looming over.

"Aye, ye do," he ground out. "And I have something to say about ye consorting with an outlaw."

"*Consorting?*" she snorted, her gaze narrowing. "God's blood, Mackay ... if I didn't know better, I'd think ye were jealous."

His mouth twisted at the suggestion.

Davina held his eye, her hands balling into fists at her sides. "Ye don't like it when Brogan Douglas speaks to me, do ye? And ye hate his flattery. What's wrong? Does he show ye up?"

Mackay snarled a curse in response. And then, before she knew what was happening, he hauled her into his arms and kissed her.

His mouth on hers was hard and hot.

Gasping, Davina wrenched away, her hand swiping upward. The 'crack' of her palm colliding with his cheek echoed through the chamber.

He jerked back, his gaze glittering, and like two opponents in the heat of battle, they stared each other down.

Like her, he was breathing hard now, his chest rising and falling sharply.

Davina should have squeezed past him then, should have made for the door—but instead, she did the opposite.

She reached forward, grabbed him by the collar of his gambeson with both hands, and yanked him close once more, going up on tiptoe to return the kiss.

Mackay stiffened in surprise. However, he recovered swiftly—and an instant later, his mouth devoured hers. Tongues, lips, and teeth clashed, and then he bent her back over his arm, one hand cradling the back of her head as he deepened the kiss further.

What started as a ferocious, angry embrace slid into something shockingly, breathlessly sensual. Davina was lost. Reaching up, she linked her arms around his neck, pulling him closer still. He tasted delicious, like fresh ale at the end of a hot summer's day, and she drank him in.

Her wits scattered, as did her thoughts. Her world narrowed to this moment. To the feel of Mackay's arms around her. To the heady taste of him. To the sensual slide of his tongue against hers. It was as if she were caught up in a whirlpool.

Mackay came to his senses first.

Still holding her fast in his arms, he lifted his mouth from hers and straightened up. Then, the rasp of their breathing filling the chamber, his gaze found hers.

Staring up at him, Davina fought the urge to wrap her arms around his neck once more, to yank his mouth down to hers. But as the moments slid by, the madness that had caught her up in its thrall cleared.

Her skin prickled, heat washing over her. *What am I doing? I'm about to become a postulant.*

Mackay's dark-blue eyes glinted as he stared down at her. His cheeks had flushed, and his lips were swollen from the violence of their kisses. "Maybe ye are right, Davina," he said hoarsely. "Perhaps, I *am* jealous. But the fact remains that assisting the likes of Brogan Douglas could cause clan Campbell to be dragged into the conflict between the Stewarts and the Douglases."

"But *ye* also assisted him," she reminded him softly, her voice catching. "Ye saved his life."

His brow furrowed. "Aye." There was no mistaking the regret in his voice. "But that was before I knew who he was."

He gently released her then and stepped away.

Cool air rushed in between them, and Davina started to tremble. She clenched her knees together to stop herself from staggering.

Mackay didn't seem to notice, for he now was heading for the door. Reaching it, he glanced over his shoulder. The captain's gaze was shuttered, even if his face was still flushed. "Ye have a stubborn, passionate nature, Davina," he said, his voice roughening slightly. "It makes me wonder if ye will be suited to a life of quiet contemplation."

An instant later, he was gone, and Davina found herself staring at the closed door.

Heart still pounding, she raised a hand to her bee-stung mouth. She could still taste him, still smell him—

and her traitorous body still yearned for him. However, her sanity had returned, and mortification prickled across her skin like a legion of marching ants. Her legs did give way under her then, and she sank down onto the bed.

Clenching her hands together, she was tempted to whisper a prayer to God, a plea to deliver her from temptation.

But it was far too late for that.

Leaving Davina's bedchamber, Lennox strode down the hallway toward the stairs. The urge to break into a run pulsed through him, although he fought it.

He wouldn't let himself flee from a woman.

Another part of him, the part that he fought just as hard, wanted to turn around and race back in there, to yank her back into his arms and claim her mouth with his again. And not stop there either.

When Davina Campbell had kissed him, feral hunger had punched him in the guts. She met him with a passion that drove him wild. He hadn't been able to think straight, and for a few moments, he'd given in to the madness.

But somewhere, deep inside, he'd eventually clawed back his wits.

Davina was his charge, his responsibility. He captained her father's guard. It was a position of trust, and all of them knew what had happened to the last man who'd breached it.

And the truth was, he wasn't just angry with her, but with himself.

He *had* been the one to step in to stop that fight today. If Brogan Douglas had ended up staying in the same inn as them, it was his fault, not Davina's.

All it had taken was a look from her, and he'd rushed forward to intercede.

Raking a hand through his short hair, he cursed. *What's wrong with ye, man?* Since when had he let a woman get to him like this?

Lennox took the rickety stairs down to the common room. And as he did so, his left cheek still tingled from the hard slap she'd delivered. He'd deserved that, had taken advantage of their proximity in the most callous fashion. And even though she'd ended up kissing him back, he knew he couldn't pretend it had never happened.

He'd overstepped, and he'd been rude to her.

He had to put things right.

The mood was strained at the table. The three of them sat there: Davina, Mackay, and Douglas. The rest of the Campbell party was seated a couple of yards away. It was busy in the common room this eve, filled with hard-drinking fishermen. A group of them were singing raucously near the open doors to the inn.

Davina cast a glance over at where Hamish and the other warriors were eating their suppers and chatting amongst themselves. Hamish caught her eye and favored Davina with a smile and a nod. Yet he ignored his captain.

Turning her attention back to their table, Davina focused on her meal. The supper was good: fried flounder and fresh oaten bread, washed down with cool ale. It was a hot, stuffy evening, and outdoors the sun was setting in a blaze of pink and gold over the sea. As always, Oban was a bonnie spot.

In the past, Davina would have lingered here a day or two, and taken rides up the coast in between exploring the busy market that took place every morning on the quayside. But with her escape from her old life awaiting, and the events of the past days unsettling her, she was relieved they would depart with the dawn.

Taking a bite of the delicate white fish, Davina cast a quick, veiled glance in Mackay's direction. They'd both avoided each other's gaze ever since taking a seat in the common room. It was awkward sitting at the same table as him, but to move elsewhere would only draw attention to what had happened upstairs. Embarrassment burned within her whenever she thought about her lewd behavior.

Fortunately, Mackay wasn't looking her way; he was too busy glaring at Douglas across the table.

Davina also focused on the outlaw. He ate heartily, hunched over his supper as if afraid someone might yank it away. Finishing his meal well ahead of his two companions, Douglas then sat back with a sigh and wrapped his hands around his tankard of ale, before meeting Davina's eye. "I appreciate yer kindness, my lady," he rumbled. "Ye have my undying thanks."

Davina forced herself to smile. Mackay's brooding presence across the table was making her uncomfortable. In truth, she wished Douglas wouldn't bring the subject up. He'd pushed her into assisting him anyway, and she couldn't help but feel manipulated. She didn't want his thanks. "Tomorrow ye can make a fresh start," she answered stiffly.

Douglas nodded before he glanced down at his filthy clothing. "I reek like a billy goat," he said, a rueful edge to his voice now. "I shall bid ye good eve, for a hot bath is awaiting me in my room."

Mackay grunted, agreeing that the man did, indeed, stink.

"We won't likely see each other in the morning," Davina said as Douglas rose to his feet. "And so, I wish ye farewell now."

"Farewell, Lady Davina," he replied, bowing his head. "And all the best for yer life at Iona." He then shifted his attention to Mackay and flashed him a smile. "And farewell to *ye*, Mackay."

Davina's brow furrowed. Was she imagining it or was there a goading edge to his smile?

At the nearby table, the Campbell warriors had ceased their conversation, their gazes traveling to

Douglas. The men's faces were grim as they watched the outlaw.

Seemingly unaffected by the continuing lack of trust toward him, Douglas departed, leaving Davina and Mackay alone together at the table.

Davina took a sip of ale and wondered how long she could wait before making an excuse and retiring as well. Only pride kept her sitting there. She didn't want Mackay to think she was afraid of him. The truth of it was that shame still pulsed within her like a stoked furnace. And her belly clenched every time she remembered that forbidden embrace.

Her passionate nature was a curse—and when it came to this infuriating man, it was going to get her into trouble.

Mackay cleared his throat then. "Lady Davina," he began gruffly. "I owe ye an apology."

Davina's gaze shifted to him squarely for the first time since supper had begun. Meanwhile, at the next table, the warriors resumed their conversation. Keith had pulled out some knucklebones, and they were beginning a game. Mackay and Davina had a little privacy.

Their gazes met and held, the moment drawing out.

"I lost my temper and behaved callously," Mackay continued, his voice roughening further. It was clear that he wasn't a man used to apologizing. "And I ask yer forgiveness."

Davina sighed. "The fault wasn't entirely yers," she admitted, forcing herself to hold his eye, even as her cheeks warmed. It would be easy to let Mackay take the blame for that kiss. But they both knew the truth of it. "I also let anger get the better of me. I said things I wish I could take back ... and I'm sorry too."

10: A WORTHY CAUSE

A STRANGE MOOD settled upon Davina when she
retired to her bedchamber later that evening. Heaviness
dragged at her limbs, and a slight headache tugged at her
temples. Suddenly, she felt indescribably weary.

Alone in her room, she went to the small window and
opened the shutters. It was oppressively hot indoors, and
humid, as if a summer storm was on its way. They were
up on the second floor of the inn here, but unfortunately,
her window didn't face west, across the firth, where it
could allow in the sea breeze. Instead, she looked out
onto the wall of the building opposite. All the same, she
welcomed a little cool air.

Moving across to the door, she bolted it from the
inside. She did this for her own security, and because, as
they'd done the previous nights, the warriors had
brought her dowry upstairs. The two heavy bags now sat
in front of the cold hearth. The room was secure, for
there was a sturdy lock on the door, and Mackay was
sleeping in the room next door as an added precaution.

Davina set about readying herself for bed.

It had been strange over the last few days, not to have
her maid helping her undress and brush out her hair for
her. All her life, Davina had been waited on. But she
deliberately hadn't brought a maid with her on this
journey. She wouldn't have any servants at Iona Abbey.
There, she would have to do everything for herself. And
so, as she fumbled with the laces of her kirtle and

wriggled out of it and the léine she wore underneath, Davina reminded herself it was for the best.

She'd left her old life behind her now, or she soon would, at least.

Pulling on her night-rail, she perched on the edge of the bed and slowly brushed her hair.

The rhythmic, gentle action relaxed her, and her eyelids grew heavier by the moment. It had been another long, and unexpected, day. She didn't linger over the task. Setting her hog bristle brush aside, Davina moved across to the window.

It was still suffocatingly hot inside the bedchamber. She was sweating and so didn't draw and bolt the shutters. Instead, she left them open a few inches and latched them loosely so that a draft could enter the room. Then, she crossed to the bed, pulled back the covers, and climbed in. The ropes creaked as she shifted position and leaned across, pulling the cover down on the lantern beside her bed.

Lying back, her gaze drifting to where silvery moonlight filtered in through the gap in the shutters, Davina tried not to think about what had ignited between her and Mackay earlier. Unfortunately, now that she was alone, and had nothing else to occupy her mind, it was impossible not to recall the heat of that kiss.

Mackay had looked suitably chastised earlier, and no doubt regretted the incident as much as she did. But neither of them could undo what had been done.

A deep sigh gusted out of Davina, her eyes fluttering shut.

It struck her then, the realization tightening her belly, that she hadn't thought about Blair once all day. After that forbidden kiss, she should have been torn apart with guilt. Blair Cameron had been the love of her life, and she'd sullied his memory.

But even though Mackay aggravated her intensely, he *had* turned her head.

A full turn of the seasons had passed since the day her father cut her lover down. And for much of that time, grief had sat like a heavy stone under her breastbone.

Once it had started to lift, the need to escape her old life had risen like a tide within her.

Davina's fingers clutched at the blankets. Blair deserved to be remembered. All the same, she could feel her lover slipping from her fingers—and there was nothing she could do about it.

Both her father and Mackay didn't think Davina suited to a nun's life—and curse them, they were right. She'd known carnal intimacy, after all. Blair's death had dulled any desire, and the choice to take the veil had initially been an easy one.

But was she perhaps wavering in her resolve?

Something was wrong.

Davina jolted out of sleep to find a heavy hand pressing down upon her mouth.

Panic grasped her around the throat when she realized that a man was crouched upon the bed, his knees pinning her to the mattress.

She couldn't make out his face, for he loomed above her, his back to the moonlight flooding in through the window. The *open* window. The intruder had somehow scaled the wall outside and managed to release the catch on the shutters before climbing into her bedchamber.

Ice washed over Davina. Mother Mary save her, she was about to be raped.

She started to struggle. She writhed and flailed against her attacker, trying to get her knees up to form a barrier between them. However, her limbs were trapped underneath the covers, deliberately so. She was pinned there, helpless.

And as she continued to twist, panic beating in her chest, the man leaned in, his hot breath feathering across her ear. "I'd calm myself, if I were ye, my lady," a male voice rasped.

Davina went still, oily fear twisting in her stomach. She knew that voice. *Brogan Douglas.*

"I'm not here to ravish ye, Davina," he whispered.

Her breathing heaved. With her mouth covered, she couldn't seem to get enough air through her nose. A strange buzzing started inside her head, dizziness sweeping over her. God's blood, she was close to fainting.

"So, this is what shall happen." There was a rough edge to his whisper now. All his earlier charm was gone. "I'm going to gag ye and bind ye to this bed. And ye are going to let me. If ye don't, I will slit yer throat." Davina's breathing hitched as something cold and hard rested against her exposed throat.

A dirk-blade.

The buzzing in her head grew louder. Time slowed, and she jolted as regret barreled into her. And strangely, it wasn't to do with Blair, but her father.

I never said goodbye to Da properly. I never told him that I loved him.

How she wished her father were here right now. He'd barrel into this chamber and cut this foul bastard down. But Colin Campbell, who for all his bluster had always protected her, was far away.

He couldn't save her. No one could.

Davina was a fighter. And her first instinct was to rail against her attacker. She didn't want to be beaten. But she also knew with chilling clarity that he'd bested her and that he wasn't issuing empty threats. He'd indeed slit her throat if she didn't do as he bid.

And so, she didn't fight him, didn't struggle as he bound a length of linen around her mouth and tied her wrists to the bed's iron frame.

Only then, did he shift his weight from her.

The moonlight, which now flooded in unimpeded through the open window, caught the harsh lines of Douglas's face. Earlier, that same face had been creased in a grateful smile. But no longer.

He flashed her a harsh grin before turning and picking up the two heavy bags of coin from before the hearth.

Davina's heart started to kick against her ribs.

So, that was what the bastard was after.

Of course, he knew she was bound for Iona Abbey; and although she hadn't mentioned the riches they carried with them, he'd obviously marked the sacks of gold.

Marked them and bided his time.

God's teeth, they'd helped a criminal.

Gripping a sack under each arm, Douglas approached the bed once more. Bending over her, he whispered again in her ear. "Apologies, Davina, but it was too much of a temptation to resist. This coin will help my clan in their fight against the king." He paused then, and although Davina couldn't see his face, she sensed he was still grinning at her. "Know that yer dowry has gone to a worthy cause."

Davina's body went rigid, rage vibrating through her. She made a muffled sound, but Douglas gave a warning growl. "I *will* happily cut yer throat if ye make a squeak while I'm leaving," he warned.

She stilled, her body going as rigid as a drawn bowstring.

Douglas swiveled from her and padded softly to the door. He then carefully lifted the heavy bar and turned the lock before drawing the door open.

Davina cursed the fact that the hinges were well-oiled. Captain Mackay's room was right next to hers. He would be alerted by such a noise, but Fortuna was with Brogan Douglas tonight, for without a backward glance, he slipped silently from the chamber, pulling the door shut behind him.

Davina lay there, heart pounding, for a short while before she decided she'd take a risk. Douglas would be well out of earshot now; she had to alert Mackay and the others to what had happened.

But when she tried to cry out, the sound was muffled. She then bucked against her restraints, kicking her legs free of the blankets. The bed was a sturdy one. It was also well away from the wall, and it didn't matter how much she flailed around, she couldn't seem to budge the bed or make much noise at all.

Tears of helpless frustration stung her eyelids as she continued to thrash and make strangled noises. But the silence around her continued, and no one heard her.

Hamish thundered up the stairs toward Lennox. "One of the horses is missing, Captain," he greeted him tersely.

Halting, Lennox cursed. The innkeeper here had agreed to keep their horses stabled till they returned from Iona. He'd assured them that the inn was secure. How the devil had someone managed to steal one of their horses? "Which one?"

"Yers."

Lennox swore once more before glancing over his shoulder. He expected Davina to appear at any moment, but he hadn't heard any movement in her room when he'd exited his just moments before. "Are the men ready?" he asked.

Hamish nodded. His expression was veiled. During this journey, Lennox had felt a slight thawing between him and the older warrior. Hamish held a lot of sway amongst the guard, and Lennox had often thought that if Hamish warmed toward him, the others would follow. Nonetheless, there was a wariness to his expression once more.

Irritation spiked through Lennox. When were these men going to accept him?

"Well, we can't worry about the missing horse now," he muttered. "We've got a boat to catch." He turned on his heel and started back up the stairs. "I'll see what's keeping Lady Davina."

He retraced his steps back to the second floor of the inn and to Davina's room, where he knocked on the door. "My lady," he called out. "Are ye ready?"

Silence followed.

He knocked again. "Lady Davina?"

Still nothing. Frowning, Lennox leaned closer to the door. His ears strained to catch the sounds from within, yet he didn't hear anything. Surely, the woman wasn't still asleep? So far on the journey, Davina had been the first of all of them to emerge from her chamber in the morning. She knew they were taking an early boat to Iona. Wasn't she in a hurry to be on her way?

Unease tickled the back of Lennox's neck. Something was amiss.

He tried the door and was surprised to find it unlocked. His brow creased. He'd warned her to bolt the door every night. Why hadn't she?

He threw the door open. The early dawn light filtered in through the window as Lennox surveyed the bedchamber.

Alarm jolted through him when he spied Colin Campbell's daughter lying on her bed, gagged and bound. Her night-rail was bunched up, indecently high on her thighs, and her eyes were wide and wild.

Three long strides brought him across the room to Davina's side, and moments later, he'd stripped the gag off and deftly released her wrists.

Davina's face was red, her cheeks streaked with tears. But her eyes were glassy with fury. "It was Douglas," she choked out. "He's taken my dowry."

Lennox's heart thudded, and he glanced over his shoulder at the space before the hearth, where the sacks of coins should have sat. However, he swiftly turned back to Davina. A dowry could be replaced, but some things were far more precious.

"Lass," he ground out. "Did he hurt ye?"

A crimson haze dropped over his vision then, rage igniting like a torch in his gut. The thought of Brogan Douglas raping her made him want to hunt the man down and give him a slow, painful death.

The intensity of Lennox's reaction shocked him, as did his protectiveness over Davina. Fury tied up his guts in knots—but relief barreled into him when she shook her head.

11: I TRUST FEW FOLK

DAVINA WALKED STIFFLY along the pier, to where the birlinn waited. Breathing was difficult this morning; it felt as if an iron band had fastened around her ribs and was slowly squeezing tight.

Glancing behind her, she spied Fergus and Elliot following; the two men bore her saddle bags. Mackay brought up the rear, his expression thunderous. The other three of their party had ridden off after Douglas. They'd discovered that he'd headed north out of Oban, presumably toward the Highlands. It was no surprise that he'd stolen Mackay's courser, the fastest of all their horses. And he would ride as if all the demons of hell were pursuing him to get to safety.

Hot anger churned through Davina then, curdling her stomach. She hated feeling so helpless. Hated that she'd been unable to stop Douglas from robbing her and that she'd been taken in by him.

Her attention rested on Captain Mackay then. Ever since he'd discovered Davina in that humiliating position earlier, trussed up like a goose at market on the bed with her night-rail around her hips, she'd struggled to meet his eye. Of course, as she'd thrashed around on the bed, trying to make a noise so someone would come to her aid, her night-rail had ridden up—and with her wrists bound to the bed, she couldn't push the garment back down.

But Mackay's gaze hadn't been lecherous, just concerned. After he'd untied her, she'd expected him to blame her for Douglas's treachery.

But he hadn't.

A muscle feathered in his jaw as he approached her. "Are ye sure about this, Davina?" he asked quietly when he reached her side.

Drawing in a shuddering breath, she nodded. She'd lost the riches she needed to give the abbess of Iona, but they were departing, nonetheless. Davina had nowhere else to go, and she was determined to use all her powers of persuasion to convince the abbess to accept her.

The events of the past days had shaken her, but she wouldn't be swayed. More than ever, Iona represented an escape—a chance to reinvent herself. Aye, she lacked the piety and reserve necessary to become a good nun, yet she'd learn. She was determined to.

Managing a brave smile, Davina patted the fine amber brooch pinned to the breast of her kirtle. "Douglas might have robbed me of my dowry, but I still have one or two items of worth left," she replied before her hand moved to the coin purse at the waist. It contained a few gold and silver pennies.

Mackay's brows drew together. "Will it be enough?"

"It has to be," she replied firmly. "Surely, when the abbess hears of what has befallen me, she'll show mercy?"

The captain's brows arched then, and Davina scowled, daring him to disagree with her.

Closing the remaining distance to the waiting birlinn, she cursed her bad luck. Ever since departing Kilchurn, things had gone from bad to worse. This had been an ill-fated journey indeed. Surely, nothing else could go wrong?

"Finally," the birlinn captain greeted her curtly when she reached the boat. Behind him, his crew was readying the galley for departure. "I was beginning to think ye weren't coming."

"Apologies, but we were delayed," Davina replied.

The captain, a big weather-beaten man, cast his gaze over the three men accompanying her. "I thought there were seven of ye?"

"There were," Mackay said, his tone clipped. "But some of our party have been detained."

The sailor frowned. "It'll still cost ye the same. Payment upfront."

Davina frowned at the man's mercenary attitude. Yet Mackay merely stepped forward, dug into his coin purse, and withdrew two silver pennies. "Half now … and half when ye have delivered me and my friends back at Oban," he said.

The captain's frown deepened, yet the uncompromising edge to Mackay's voice must have warned him that it wasn't a good idea to quibble.

Mouth pursed, the captain tucked the coins away. "Very well," he grumbled. "Get on board then."

Standing at the bow of the birlinn, Davina looked ahead to where the Isle of Mull shadowed the northwestern sky. She didn't look back at the mainland, didn't glance over at her companions.

Instead, she focused on their destination: the Isle of Iona lay just off the western shore of Mull.

The galley slid across the firth, propelled by oars at first, and then—when the birlinn's single sail billowed— by a stiff, salty breeze. It was another warm morning, yet there was a weight to the air, warning that the weather was close to turning. Indeed, clouds billowed across the wide sky, and those forming to the west had a threatening edge to them.

Wrapping her arms about her torso and shivering, Davina blinked as spindrift settled over her in a fine mist. She'd grown up on the coast for a time, before her father had started work on Kilchurn Castle, and loved the tang of the briny air. It reminded her of happier times, and although Loch Awe was beautiful, she'd missed the changing moods of the coast.

At Iona, she'd be surrounded by the wild sea.

Davina's breathing grew shallow. She had to ensure they admitted her.

"My lady." A man's voice roused her then, and Davina tore her attention from the sea to where Captain Mackay stood at her shoulder. She hadn't realized he'd moved up to the bow. Ever since their kiss, he'd been formal and respectful with her, almost painfully so.

"Yes, Captain," she replied stiffly.

"Are ye well?"

She met his gaze. "Why wouldn't I be?"

His mouth pursed. "A rogue gagged and tied ye to yer bed ... ye must have feared for yer life last night."

Davina swallowed, her pulse quickening as she recalled the terror that had twisted like a living thing within her. "Aye," she admitted huskily. "He held a blade to my throat and threatened to kill me if I made a sound ... I believe he would have."

Mackay's features tightened. "If I ever set eyes on Douglas again, I shall gut him," he said. His voice was low and hard, and she didn't doubt him. Even so, his vehemence took her aback. She'd thought she merely exasperated him. Did he care what happened to her?

They continued to stare at each other, the moments drawing out.

Davina's breathing quickened. Hades, it was still there, the powerful pull between them. If she let herself, she could drown in those dark-blue eyes.

Swallowing once more, Davina tore her gaze from his and focused on the glassy waves the birlinn cut through.

It was just as well their journey together was ending, for it was dangerous to spend any more time with Lennox Mackay.

When she finally spied the Isle of Iona on the horizon, the nerves that had already tied Davina's stomach in knots twisted.

This wasn't going to be easy, yet she was determined.

She wasn't naïve enough to believe that the abbess would instantly overlook her lack of dowry and admit her into the abbey. If it were that easy to gain entry, every homeless woman from the Orkneys to Hadrian's Wall would make the pilgrimage to the isle and beg sanctuary. Only the daughters of the wealthy ended up here—and Davina knew she'd have to work hard to plead her case.

And she would.

The isle was small, rocky, and green, yet bare of trees. White sandy beaches glinted in the noon sun, and as they drew closer, she spied the grey bulk of the abbey rising against the sky. It sat back from a pebbly shore and a wooden pier.

Even from a distance, Davina could sense the serenity of this island. It lay apart from the cares of the rest of the world. Her heart started to thud against her breastbone then. It was the refuge she'd been searching for.

They moored at the pier, the only boat there.

"How long will ye be?" the birlinn captain asked Mackay once his passengers had disembarked. He motioned then to the west, where the sky gradually grew darker. "I'd prefer to be back at Oban before the weather worsens."

"This shouldn't take long," Mackay replied, his tone curt. He then glanced at Fergus and Elliot. "Wait here, lads. I shall escort Lady Davina up to the abbey."

Both warriors nodded, their gazes wary as they eyed their captain.

Indeed, the look that passed between Mackay and his men warned Davina that he didn't trust the birlinn captain not to set sail without them if given the chance.

Nonetheless, he'd forfeit the rest of his promised fare if he did that.

Mackay threw a saddlebag over each shoulder and led the way off the boat.

"Ye don't trust him, do ye?" Davina murmured to her companion as they climbed the path toward the abbey. Its high walls loomed above, stark against the sky.

Mackay cut her a wry look. "As ye have already seen, I trust few folk."

Davina arched an eyebrow. His assertion didn't come as a surprise. She'd marked the cynical comments he'd made during the journey. He'd been nakedly suspicious of Brogan Douglas too, although his instinct about him had been right. Davina hadn't trusted the outlaw either, yet his pushiness and compliments had swayed her. She now wished she hadn't let politeness override good sense.

It wasn't a mistake she'd make again.

Curiosity wreathed up then. She and Mackay were about to part ways, but a fascination for him had sparked and was steadily growing. She knew very little about the man who led her father's guard, and wished now that she'd asked him about the life he'd left behind. "And why is that?" she asked after a beat.

His mouth quirked. "Life is easier that way."

12: AT THE GATE

THE ABBESS CAME out to meet them at the gate.

Of course, Lennox hadn't expected to be given access—he was a man, after all—but he'd hoped the nuns might let Davina enter the abbey alone.

They didn't.

Abbess Anna was a tall woman of around forty winters. She had well-drawn features and might have been considered pretty if her expression hadn't been so stern. The black tunic and veil, and the white wimple that surrounded her face, removed all traces of femininity from her. The woman's face and hands were the only skin she revealed to the world.

Earlier, Lennox had rung a bell and waited until a small wooden shutter pulled back and a reserved female voice enquired who was calling. Davina had asked to speak to the abbess on a matter of great importance, and the shutter had whispered closed.

It had taken Abbess Anna a while to respond—but here she was. Two small terriers had followed her outdoors, and the dogs now played behind her, their growls drifting across the compound as they fought over a scrap of bone.

Ignoring the noise, the abbess cast a cool look over the man and woman standing before her. "How can I help ye?"

Davina stepped forward, her head bowed in respect. "Reverend Mother. My name is Lady Davina Campbell, daughter of the Lord of Glenorchy ... and I am here to request entrance as a postulant into this order."

A brief silence followed before the abbess replied. "I had no word from yer father of this."

"No, Reverend Mother. The decision was taken quickly ... there was no time to send a letter ahead."

Lennox's gaze shifted between Davina and the abbess. The older woman was observing Colin Campbell's daughter with interest. But that was to be expected—for she hadn't heard the rest yet.

Lennox admired Davina's determination, although on the boat ride here, he'd refrained from pointing out that he didn't hold much hope that she'd gain entry to Iona—not without those two bags of coin.

Davina had a hard enough task before her as it was without him dampening her spirits.

"We brought a fine dowry from Kilchurn Castle," Davina said, keeping her gaze bowed. "But yestereve, in Oban, I was robbed. Now, I have nothing but a small purse of coin and this brooch." She reached up, her finger stroking the amber that gleamed gold in the sunlight. She paused then. "It belonged to my mother, a Maclean, like ye, Reverend Mother."

The abbess inclined her head, while her expression had shuttered. "Is that so?"

"Aye, we are second cousins, I believe."

Lennox fought a smile. Davina was a wily one. He wondered if that was the truth; even so, it was a clever ploy. If Campbell's daughter could appeal to this woman's compassion, and clan loyalty, she might just overlook her lack of dowry.

But Abbess Anna didn't comment on their kinship. Instead, she huffed a sigh. "That is ill news indeed about ye being robbed."

"Aye, Reverend Mother," Lennox spoke up then. "A man we rescued from brigands on the road ended up betraying our trust."

The abbess's gaze snapped to him, her blue eyes narrowing. "Can ye not hunt him down?"

"Three of my men are doing so as we speak ... but he got a head start on us and has headed north."

The abbess shook her head slowly, her mouth pursing. She then turned her attention back to Davina. "Ye have been unfortunate indeed, my child," she said softly. "And I wish I could welcome ye. But without a dowry, I cannot."

Lennox stilled, while beside him, he heard Davina's swift intake of breath. "I will work hard," she assured the abbess huskily, "and be a credit to this order."

"Of that, I have no doubt ... but if I break the rules for one, others will follow." The abbess paused then and shook her head once more. "We live in isolation here and rely on the patronage of clan-chiefs and chieftains to survive. If I start accepting postulants without dowries, we shall be overrun."

Lennox's mouth thinned at this flimsy excuse. That wasn't the real reason. The truth was that for all their talk of abstinence and austerity, the church hoarded its riches. It loved gold and silver as much as everyone else.

"Reverend Mother." Davina sank to her knees then, her hands coming up to clasp before her.

The sight made Lennox's pulse quicken. He didn't like to see Davina like this. Her voice had cracked then, revealing her desperation. He wanted to step forward, haul her to her feet, and tell her that she kneeled to no one—but that wouldn't help matters.

And so, he watched as Davina started to plead with the abbess. "I beg ye to grant me yer compassion and mercy." The words tumbled out of her. "To make one exception."

"Perhaps ye can return home and collect another dowry, my child," the abbess replied, irritation creeping into her voice now. She wasn't appreciating Davina's display. "We will speak again then."

"My father emptied his coffers to give ye such an offering, Reverend Mother," Davina replied.

"The Lord of Glenorchy will not be short of funds, I'm sure," Abbess Anna sniffed. Meanwhile, her dogs started yapping as they now chased each other around the yard.

Davina looked up into the abbess's face, tears glittering in her eyes. "He has washed his hands of me," she whispered.

The abbess's tall frame stiffened. "And why would that be?"

Lennox's pulse quickened further. Christ's teeth, why had Davina mentioned that? Abbess Anna was looking for a reason to deny her, and she'd just handed one over.

Realizing this, Davina dropped her gaze once more. Tears trickled down her cheeks, and something deep inside Lennox twisted. Davina didn't deserve this humiliation.

"I refused to take a husband ... and he lost his patience. He has cast me out. I have nowhere else to go."

The abbess's finely drawn eyebrows arched. "I have the feeling there is more to this tale than ye are telling me. Unfortunately, I'm not here to provide refuge from family squabbles. Not once during yer pleas have ye mentioned yer piety, yer devotion to the Lord. Ye will have to return home and throw yerself at yer father's mercy." She gave a heavy, irritated sigh then and stepped back, making it clear that she didn't wish to continue the conversation. "I wish ye a safe journey home, my child. May the Lord bless ye and keep ye."

And then, with a swish of heavy robes, Abbess Anna turned, called to her terriers—who took off yipping excitedly across the compound—and strode back inside the abbey.

A moment later, the heavy wooden gate swung shut in their faces.

Silence fell, broken only by the whine of the rising wind around them—and then Davina covered her face with her hands and started weeping in earnest.

Lennox watched her for a moment, his gut clenching, before he moved.

He couldn't bear it. He couldn't let her cry as if her heart were breaking.

Shifting close, he slid his hands under Davina's arms and lifted her to her feet. The feat was an easy one, for she was slender and as light as a child. Sobs shook her body as he put his arms around her and pulled her close, letting her weep against his chest.

Under normal circumstances, he was sure Davina would have shoved him away and torn strips off him for being so bold. But such was her upset, she merely clung to him, as if he were a rock and she were drowning.

And there they stood, the wind eddying around them and snagging at their clothing.

Lennox didn't speak. There was nothing he could say to ease Davina's upset. All he could do was hold her and wait for the storm to pass.

She would be disappointed, for she'd been pinning all her hopes on beginning a new life at Iona Abbey. But fate clearly had other plans for Davina Campbell. It seemed she wasn't meant to be a nun.

Lennox cast a dark look at the closed gate. That woman could have bent the rules for her, yet she wouldn't be moved.

"Come, lass," he said eventually as Davina's sobs quietened. Her face was buried against his gambeson; he could feel the dampness of her tears soaking through it and the léine he wore underneath, yet he didn't mind. On the contrary, it felt strangely right—as if she belonged in his arms.

Panic jolted through Lennox at this realization, and he gently drew back, pushing her away from him. Maybe holding her like this wasn't a good idea, after all. It roused sensations he didn't know how to deal with.

Davina sniffed loudly before reaching up with a shaking hand and wiping at her wet, flushed cheeks. "I'm sorry," she rasped. "I don't know what came over me. I don't usually make such a display."

"Ye were disappointed," he replied, resisting the urge to reach out and brush away the tears that still trickled down her face. "That's all."

"The abbess is right," she admitted roughly, glancing across at the closed gate. "I'm not devout enough."

Lennox's lips pursed. "I fear that was but an excuse, Davina," he replied, unable to prevent skepticism from rising in his voice. "It's the gold she cares about, not yer piety."

Davina's gaze met his, her eyes glittering. "Maybe ye are right," she murmured.

Lennox sighed. "Let's go down to the pier," he said gently, putting an arm about her shoulders and steering her away from the abbey. "There's no point in remaining here."

Davina nodded. Stumbling at his side, she allowed Lennox to lead her down to the water.

"Well?" the birlinn captain greeted them, his gaze traveling from Lennox to Davina. "I take it things didn't go well?"

Lennox shook his head. He then glanced over at where Fergus and Elliot were watching him. Meeting Fergus's eye, Lennox's mouth curved into a humorless smile. "Lady Davina is coming back with us."

13: I'M NEVER GOING BACK THERE

IT WAS A rough journey back to Oban, for the wind had picked up. The waves had turned huge and glassy, and all the passengers were forced to remain seated, clinging to the sides as the birlinn rode the swells.

Both Fergus and Elliot were violently sick, heaving up their guts over the edge of the boat. Lennox also battled with nausea but managed to swallow down bile as he crouched next to Davina.

The lady herself wore a miserable expression. Her thin face was pinched, her throat convulsing as she grasped his arm with each roll of the boat.

Meanwhile, the captain and his men moved around the birlinn, trimming the sail and maneuvering the galley back to shore. The port was in view when the storm finally hit in its full screeching fury.

Despite that it was mid-summer, icy needles of rain peppered Lennox's face. Around them, the sky turned purple, and lightning lit up the heavens while thunder boomed overhead.

The birlinn tossed in the huge swells, freezing water crashing over the bow and dousing them all.

By the time they reached Oban, Fergus and Elliot were ghostly pale, their hair plastered against their skulls. Likewise, Lennox and Davina were soaked through.

Paying the birlinn captain, they disembarked onto the storm-swept quay, hauling Davina's bags with them. Heads bent against the howling wind, as waves crashed against the docks, the party hurried out of the tempest, along the quayside to the inn.

As Lennox expected, Hamish and the others hadn't yet returned—so, Lennox arranged lodgings for the night. He also requested a hot bath be drawn for Davina in her chamber.

She was shivering as he led her upstairs, and he worried she might have caught a chill during the journey back from Iona. Inside her chamber, he set down the saddlebags by the bed, while two lads carried in a large iron tub, followed by lasses bearing buckets of hot water.

Davina perched on the edge of the bed as others moved around her. She hadn't spoken since leaving Iona, and her quietness bothered him.

Lennox hunkered down before her and took hold of her hands. They were delicate and freezing cold.

Gently chafing them between his own hands, he met her gaze. "I shall leave ye to bathe, Davina," he murmured. "A lass will bring ye up some supper in an hour."

She nodded wordlessly.

Lennox held her eye. "Are ye feeling unwell?"

"No," she replied huskily. "Just a little queasy from that rough ride." She then managed a wan smile. "I'm sure I'll feel better after a hot bath."

Lennox nodded, relieved. "Right then." He released her hands and rose to his feet. "I will let ye be." He moved toward the door.

"Lennox."

He halted and glanced back at Davina. "Aye?"

She managed another tremulous smile. "Thank ye."

Entering the common room, Lennox found it full of ill-tempered men in oilskins: fishermen who were discussing how long the foul weather would last. The innkeeper had lit the hearth, and the humid air was heavy with the odor of wet wool.

Spying Elliot and Fergus seated at a table near the stairs, Lennox made his way across to them.

Fergus met his eye. "How is Lady Davina, Captain?"

"Better," he replied, falling into a chair and raking a hand through his damp hair.

"Nothing a hot bath won't cure, eh?" Elliot said hopefully.

Lennox pulled a face. He certainly hoped so, although after seeing how upset Davina was on Iona, her disappointment at being refused entry to the abbey, he wasn't so sure.

Her admission that she wasn't pious hadn't come as a shock. As he'd already told her, she wouldn't make a good nun—her sensuality aside, Davina was too willful and independent to be trapped in such a life.

No, she'd been seeking to hide on Iona, to run from her mistakes and her oppressive father.

A serving lass approached their table then, and Lennox ordered the three of them meals and tankards of ale. Elliot and Fergus were still looking a little peaky after their rough boat ride, yet they'd recover soon enough.

The two men had previously said little to their captain, but the day's events had made them lose some of their reserve. It was rare that Lennox ever ate with them, and when the plates of roast mutton and fresh bread arrived, he enjoyed their company. Later, when Fergus pulled out a pouch of knucklebones, he happily played a few games with them.

He'd missed this—the easy camaraderie between warriors. As captain, he'd felt as if he was apart from his men. In the past, he'd envied his brother Kerr his position as Captain of the Dun Ugadale Guard. But did he too find it a lonely position?

"What will Lady Davina do now, Captain?" Elliot asked finally, as he took his turn with the knucklebones, scattering them across the sticky tabletop.

"I imagine it all depends on whether Hamish and the lads manage to catch up with Douglas," Lennox answered. His mood darkened. The thought that

Douglas might escape made Lennox's gut ache. "If they recover her dowry, we can take her back to Iona." His mouth pursed. "The abbess won't turn her away if she comes bearing coin."

"And if they don't catch him?" Fergus asked, eying Lennox over the rim of his tankard. They were onto their third round now, and the ale had loosened all their tongues.

"I suppose we'll have to take her back to Kilchurn," Elliot replied, his brow furrowing.

Lennox nodded, although the tension in his stomach wound tighter at the thought. Campbell had made his position clear the night before they departed Kilchurn. If his daughter departed for Iona, she would be dead to him.

He wouldn't want her back.

Seated in the bath, knees drawn up under her chin, Davina stared at the wall.

God's bones, she'd made a mess of things. Her breathing grew shallow, and her eyes burned at the memory of the humiliating encounter with the abbess. And then, to shame herself further, she'd fallen to pieces before the gate of the abbey. Mackay held her while she sobbed against his chest, but no doubt he thought her hysterical, unhinged.

She'd caused him nothing but trouble ever since leaving Kilchurn.

Muttering an oath, she leaned her forehead on her knees. Around her, steam and the woodsy smell of rosemary from the scented oil one of the lasses had added drifted up. It comforted Davina a little, a reminder of her mother's herb garden at their old broch.

"What will I do now, Ma?" she whispered, wishing her mother were here to advise her. "I can't go home."

She'd put all her hopes into being admitted to Iona, yet the way was now barred.

Of course, Hamish, Archie, and Keith might catch up with that Douglas villain. They might return with the riches he'd robbed. But even as the hope fluttered up, so did despair.

Brogan Douglas was desperate, and desperate men weren't easily caught.

"We tracked him east and then north, along the shore of Loch Etive, Captain ... but when he turned into the mountains, we lost him."

Hamish's gruff words fell like hammer blows within the bedchamber.

"Aye," Keith muttered. "We followed the bastard across the foothills of Ben Starav before he vanished like a wraith."

Davina's gaze swept across the faces of the three men gathered before her. She'd been seated by the fire, listening to rain pattering on the shutters, when Mackay knocked on her door, announcing that the men he'd sent after Douglas had returned.

A short while later, all the warriors escorting her had marched into the chamber. However, her gaze had seized upon those he sent after the outlaw.

They were sweaty and dirty and haggard with exhaustion. It was obvious Hamish, Keith, and Archie had pursued Brogan Douglas hard, but he'd still managed to elude them like the slippery eel he was. Of course, he'd had a good head start. Even weighed down by heavy coin, he'd gotten away.

"So, that's it then," she said after a weighty pause. "My dowry really is gone."

"Aye," Hamish replied, his voice rough with disappointment. "I'm sorry, Lady Davina ... I've failed ye."

Davina shook her head. "None of this is yer doing, Hamish. Ye did yer best."

Despair pressed down upon her shoulders as she spoke. Nearly four days had passed since Douglas had robbed her. She'd spent much of her time alone in this chamber, waiting for news, while secretly knowing how it would end.

Hamish huffed a weary sigh. "Shall we depart for Kilchurn in the morning then, my lady?"

Silence fell in the chamber, broken only by the soft crackle of the hearth. The rain had lowered the summery temperatures and damp crept in. Yet the warmth of the fire couldn't thaw the lump of ice that had taken up residence in Davina's belly.

"No," she whispered eventually, shifting her gaze to the flickering flames. "I'm never going back there ... I can't."

Another pause followed before Mackay cleared his throat. "Perhaps we can take ye to relatives, Lady Davina ... do ye have kin living nearby?"

Davina drew in a deep breath before glancing his way. Mackay stood, leaning up against the mantelpiece, arms folded across his chest. His brow was furrowed as he watched her.

"I have no one else," she replied.

"But what about yer uncle at Castle Gloom?" Hamish asked. The big man was scowling now.

Davina shook her head. "Angus Campbell ... and his sons ... are vile bullies," she replied, suppressing a shiver. "I would never throw myself at his mercy."

Indeed, she'd never forget the unpleasant summers spent at Castle Gloom, perched high above rocky gorges, as a child—or the way the eldest of her cousins had tormented her with spiders.

"But there has to be somewhere ye could go, my lady?" Fergus said, his voice tight with concern. "We can't leave ye here."

Davina's gaze swept around the chamber, taking in the worried faces of her escort. They were all good men, and she was sorry to have put them in such an awkward position.

"Ye must," she said finally. "I have enough coin left in my purse to pay for lodgings and meals for a short while ... I will look for work as a laundress ... or serving ale in a local tavern." Nonetheless, as she spoke these words, dread curled under Davina's ribs. Whom was she trying to fool? She wasn't altogether useless, yet she'd been brought up in a sheltered environment. She'd never washed a garment in her life or served anyone ale but her father.

A stony silence followed these words, and the aghast look on the warriors' faces told her they knew the truth of it. She wouldn't survive long on her own.

Davina's throat constricted then, and she swallowed hard to loosen it.

Eventually, Lennox Mackay answered. "Leaving ye here is out of the question, my lady," he said firmly.

Davina's lips parted as she readied herself to argue with him. The decisions she'd made over the past years had led her to this point. Her life was unraveling before her eyes, yet she'd find a way out of this mess—even if it meant scrubbing floors for a living. It was time to swallow her pride.

But Mackay continued before she could speak. "It's a terrible shame yer relationship with yer father has deteriorated so far. I understand why ye cannot return to Kilchurn ... but if ye will not go to yer kin at Castle Gloom, I see only one solution." He paused then, his gaze seizing hers. "I shall take ye to *my* family upon the Kintyre peninsula ... they will take care of ye."

14: ON A KNIFE EDGE

SILENCE ECHOED THROUGH the bedchamber. It was as quiet as a chapel, and all eyes were on Lennox.

Swallowing to ease the sudden tightness in his throat, and the panic that was bubbling up, Lennox ignored them all save Davina.

Her reaction was the only one that mattered.

He couldn't believe he'd just made that offer. He hadn't planned it—and in fact, if he'd considered the idea earlier, he'd have talked himself out of it. But now that the words had left his mouth, he couldn't call them back.

And as his gaze held Davina's, he found he didn't want to. Somehow, this decision felt like the right one.

He knew it, deep in the marrow of his bones.

Davina Campbell didn't look as convinced—and neither did his men.

"Mackay," Hamish muttered, dragging a hand down his face. "Have ye lost yer wits?"

Lennox shook his head. "No, I'm using them to find a solution to our lady's predicament."

"Ye are kind indeed to offer me sanctuary amongst yer clan, Captain," Davina said, her voice husky. "But yer brother might not be as welcoming as ye believe."

Lennox smiled. "Iver Mackay will not turn away a woman in need," he said as warmth suffused his chest. Aye, his brother was a good man—the best of them in many ways. "Ye know he is recently wed, and his wife, Bonnie, will want a companion her own age. They will *all* welcome ye. Ye will be safe at Dun Ugadale, protected."

And as he said these words, Lennox believed them.

Even on the last occasion he'd seen his brother, in the courtyard of Kilchurn, Iver had told him he'd always be welcome at Dun Ugadale. At the time, Lennox hadn't cared, for he'd been determined to carve a new path for himself, away from his family. The brothers' relationship had grown strained over the past years, and Iver had been hurt by Lennox's decision to take up the position at Kilchurn. But he hadn't burned any bridges as he'd left Lennox behind.

Aye, it would be a blow to Lennox's pride to return to Dun Ugadale and ask this of his brother—but he'd do it. And not just for Davina, but for himself.

It's time to go home.

The realization made his pulse quicken. He couldn't lie to himself any longer. Dun Ugadale was where he belonged.

Lennox turned his attention then to his men. They were all watching him with a mix of disbelief—and something else. Was he imagining it, or was there warmth in their eyes as they regarded him, respect? After months of standoffishness, of following orders under sufferance, the men he led had finally accepted him.

"Colin Campbell won't like this," Hamish pointed out then.

"I doubt he'll care," Davina murmured. Yet her gaze never shifted from Lennox. "I'm dead to him, remember?"

"Aye, but that doesn't mean he won't have an opinion on where ye end up," Hamish replied, folding heavily muscled arms across his chest.

Lennox was inclined to agree with him.

"It's best ye tell Campbell that taking Lady Davina to Dun Ugadale was wholly my idea," he advised him. "I will escort the lady to my brother's broch, while the rest of ye return to Kilchurn. When ye see Campbell, tell him that she will be well looked after."

"And what about ye, Captain?" Hamish's heavy brow furrowed. "Will ye follow us home after leaving Lady Davina at Dun Ugadale?"

A pause followed. "No," he replied. "It's best ye let Campbell know that he will need to find himself another captain." Lennox glanced at Davina once more. She was still observing him. Her expression was veiled, yet her eyes were bright.

There was something in her look that unnerved him. Over the past few days, the woman had revealed that she saw what others didn't. Lennox found it difficult to hide from her; somehow, she always pierced his defenses.

"Of course, the choice is yers, my lady," he said, his mouth lifting at the corners. He hated the idea of her remaining here in Oban to scratch a living—but the final word had to come from her. "Will ye come with me to Dun Ugadale?"

Their stare drew out, and Lennox began to wonder if she would decline. She was proud, after all. He too could be prideful and knew just how hard it was to accept help from others, even when it was well-meant.

But then her small rosebud mouth lifted into a half-smile. "Yer offer is a kind one indeed, Captain ... and only a goose-witted lass would refuse it." She paused then, her gaze warming. "I will go with ye."

"Campbell will be as vexed as a swatted hornet when he hears of this, Mackay." Hamish stepped close as Lennox finished saddling the heavyset gelding—Elliot's horse—cinching the girth tight. The gelding stomped an impatient feathered hoof, narrowly missing Lennox's foot. "He will believe ye have compromised his daughter."

Lennox glanced over his shoulder. The man's gaze gleamed in the dim light inside the stables. Dawn had just broken. Outside, it was misty and cool, yet the weather had settled. It was time for all of them to move on.

"I'm aware of that," he replied with an answering frown. "However, I trust ye will assure him that isn't the case."

"I will," Hamish rumbled. "But ye know what Colin is like. When it comes to his daughter, he doesn't see straight ... he never has. His wife only ever bore him one bairn, although he never complained about that. Davina was once the light of his life ... his wee shadow. She followed him everywhere, and he taught her how to ride, how to hunt." The warrior halted then as if embarrassed by his frankness.

"And yet he's been so harsh with her," Lennox replied.

Hamish huffed a sigh. "Aye, unfortunately, his daughter grew up. When he discovered her affair with Cameron, he felt betrayed." Hamish shook his head. "But that doesn't mean he hates his daughter ... on the contrary, perhaps he loves her *too* much."

Lennox's frown deepened. "Thank ye for the warning, Hamish," he replied. "I will write to Campbell when we arrive at Dun Ugadale, assuring him that Davina is safe and well."

The look on Hamish's face told him that wouldn't likely be enough. Nonetheless, there was nothing else Lennox could do. Campbell had washed his hands of Davina, and Lennox wouldn't let her suffer because of it.

Leading his horse out of the stables, Lennox found the rest of their party, including Davina, waiting for him. Clad in a hooded woolen cloak, her pale, heart-shaped face was set in an expression of grim resolve.

Lennox's chest tightened just a little.

He didn't want to push her into anything, but surely Davina would realize this was the best choice—the only choice?

"Are we all ready?" he asked, his gaze sweeping the amassed company.

His men had all saddled up and were ready to go. He and Davina would be riding together on Elliot's gelding, while the warrior would ride Davina's palfrey back to Kilchurn.

They nodded, although their faces were all solemn, as if they all knew there would be ramifications for this act.

Lennox understood that too. Nothing any of them did was without consequence. Like throwing a pebble into a still pond, there would be ripples—there always were. But at least this way, Davina would be spared humiliation and suffering. This way, her father would at least know that she was safe.

They left Oban without fanfare, the hollow clip-clop of their horses' hooves loud on the wet road. The company wouldn't part ways for a day at least, not until the road forked, at which point, Hamish would lead the other warriors east toward Loch Awe, while Lennox and Davina pushed south for the Kintyre peninsula.

Davina perched behind Mackay, her arms looped loosely around his waist. They rode in silence, and she was grateful that he wasn't in a chatty mood this morning.

She wished to retreat into her own thoughts, to ready herself for parting ways with the rest of her escort and accompanying Mackay to Dun Ugadale.

Nervousness fluttered in her belly, like someone had just let a sack of moths loose, whenever she dwelt on the situation.

Have I made another mistake?

She'd taken so many missteps of late that she no longer trusted her own judgment. Perhaps it would have been better to remain in Oban and swallow her pride before looking for work.

This choice could end up making things worse for her.

She was trying not to lean against Mackay as they rode, although the jolting step of their horse threw them together with every stride. His body was tense, and she could feel the determination in him.

His behavior had shocked her. Everything she thought she knew about him had been shattered the previous evening when he'd offered to take her to his kin. In doing so, he was breaking with her father and giving up his position as Captain of the Kilchurn Guard.

All to help her.

It was a far cry from his flippant manner when they'd set out from Kilchurn. Aye, they were no longer at loggerheads, as they had been, yet she hadn't expected him to make such a gesture. She wanted to question him about his decision, to assure herself that he wouldn't get into trouble for this, but she'd decided to wait until they left the others behind. Once they were traveling alone, it would be safer to speak frankly.

The day stretched on, misty and cool, and none of them said much.

They took a break at noon, eating a light meal of bread and cheese, before pushing on once more. Eventually, they stopped at Kintraw for the night.

It felt odd to see the hamlet again, for they'd stayed there on the way north. Not even a week had passed since then, yet it seemed much longer to Davina.

And as they rode into Kintraw, the party passed a large standing stone.

Mist wreathed around the tall, pitted monolith as dusk settled. Standing at least thirteen feet high, it presided over a stacked stone cairn. On the way north, one of the serving lads at the inn had told Davina that locals believed it to be the grave of a long-dead Norse prince. However, she'd been so focused on her destination that she hadn't given it much thought at the time.

Her gaze settled on the huge stone now, as they rode by, and she wondered at the man who lay buried there. Of course, Norse blood flowed through the veins of many Scots.

"Ye could be related to the man buried here, ye know?" she said, breaking the silence between her and Mackay.

He snorted a laugh in response. "Why do ye think that?"

"Well, there's no mistaking that ye bear a Norse heritage," she replied. "Yer height, high cheekbones, dark-blue eyes, and blond hair are all testament to it."

Davina's voice trailed off. Goose. Now he'd know she'd been paying close attention to him.

And she had. Mackay was a striking man indeed—the kind that no doubt set many a maid's heart aflutter. Aye, she'd noticed the appreciative looks the serving lasses in Oban had favored him with. She too found herself watching him when he thought she wasn't looking.

"Maybe ye are right, Davina," Mackay said after a brief pause, a faint teasing edge creeping into his voice. "Although my Norse blood will be well diluted by now, I'd wager."

Davina didn't reply. Instead, her cheeks warmed, and she was grateful she was sitting behind Mackay so he didn't see her reaction. Dropping the subject, she instead focused ahead on the huddle of stone houses emerging from the mist before them.

It was best she didn't talk to him in such a familiar manner, not if they were going to be traveling alone shortly. And it was also best if she forgot that heated kiss they'd shared just a few days earlier. She'd only become flustered in his presence if she dwelled upon it. She had to rein in her impulses.

Davina's future teetered on a knife edge, and recklessness of any kind could spell her ruin.

From now on, I'm not taking any risks, she told herself. *I will keep my head down and be thankful I'm not destitute.*

At Dun Ugadale, she would focus on making herself useful to the Mackays so that the laird wouldn't find her a burden.

She would leave her willfulness, and privilege, behind her.

15: LOST

THEY SAID THEIR farewells at the crossroads an hour's ride south of Kintraw the following morning.

A warm wind gusted across the hills as the five warriors who'd accompanied Davina north reined in their horses and twisted in the saddle to face her.

"Goodbye, my lady," Hamish said, favoring Davina with a tight smile. The older man's eyes were shadowed this morning. He was trying to hide it, but he was worried about her. "Take care of yerself."

"And ye too, Hamish," she replied, warmth in her voice. Her gaze then slid to each of their faces. "Keith, Archie, Fergus, and Elliot," she named each of them. "Ye are honorable men, and I will never forget yer loyalty over the years. I wish ye all well."

"Aye, my lady,'" Archie replied, clearing his throat. The red-haired warrior had flushed pink with embarrassment. "Have a safe journey to Dun Ugadale."

"Fear not, I shall take care of her, Archie," Mackay said then. He was seated in front of Davina, and as such, she couldn't see his expression. "I shall protect Lady Davina with my life."

Davina's breathing caught. There was a quiet surety in his voice, one that made her cheeks warm and her pulse start to patter. His assurance made her feel both flustered and reassured.

Yet his words pleased the others. Fergus and Elliot flashed him warm smiles, while Archie and Keith both nodded. Hamish inclined his head, his eyes crinkling at the corners as his bearded face split into a grin. "Ye're all right, Mackay," he said gruffly.

Lennox Mackay snorted a soft laugh. "Just come to that realization now, have ye?"

Hamish scratched his bearded jaw before shrugging. "I'll admit that me and the lads weren't sure about ye ... until this trip."

"But ye showed us ye don't shy away from a scrap," Fergus piped up.

"Aye ... ye've got balls," Archie added.

Davina coughed into her hand. The warriors seemed to have forgotten there was a lady present.

Archie flashed her an apologetic look, while Hamish glanced over at Mackay once more. "We're sorry to lose ye as our captain," he admitted then. "But ye are doing the right thing."

"I know," Mackay replied quietly. "Thank ye, Hamish."

The older warrior nodded before glancing over at Davina once more. "Godspeed, my lady."

Davina smiled back. "And ye."

They parted ways then.

Mackay turned his gelding and urged the heavy feather-footed beast into a swift canter, while the others headed west toward Loch Awe.

Davina was comfortable on a horse's back and had a good seat. Nonetheless, she tightened her hold on Mackay's waist just a fraction. The road was uneven, and he was setting a cracking pace.

Neither of them spoke as they traveled south, kicking up stones and dirt behind them. If Davina was honest, it felt awkward to be alone together. In other circumstances, it would have been considered improper. But after everything that had happened, her reputation no longer mattered.

She'd already disgraced herself when she embarked on an affair with Blair Cameron, and then had lost her father's love by insisting she take the veil. And now, she'd lost her dowry.

Whether or not anything improper occurred between her and Mackay, few would care now.

It already has.

Davina's belly fluttered as she recalled the heat of his mouth on hers, the passion of his kiss. She'd wanted more—they both had. But at least Mackay had stopped things before they'd gotten out of control.

Davina squeezed her eyes closed, giving herself up to the jolting rhythm of the gelding's canter. *Think of something else, lass,* she counseled herself. *Or ye shall get yerself into trouble.*

Once they'd left Kintraw far behind, Lennox eventually slowed their pace. It was a breezy day, and clouds scudded across the sky. They rode over emerald-green hills sprinkled with clover, heather, and thistles—varying hues of purple.

Lennox had been tense upon departing that morning, yet with each furlong south, something inside him unraveled.

I'm going home.

Home. Had he missed it that much? Over the last few months, he'd stubbornly fought his longing to see the moss-encrusted walls of Dun Ugadale and the windswept hills of the Kintyre peninsula. But now he didn't.

Lennox's breath grew shallow, excitement unfurling inside him.

He'd have to eat humble pie, of course—yet he'd do it.

"This is lovely countryside," Davina drew his attention then, speaking for the first time in hours.

"Aye." Lennox smiled. "It gets bleaker as ye ride south, yet there is a beauty in it."

A pause followed before she spoke once more. "Ye miss yer kin, don't ye?" Despite himself, Lennox tensed, yet she continued, "When ye spoke of yer brother yesterday, I saw it in yer eyes."

A sigh gusted out of Lennox then. "Iver and I didn't part on the best of terms," he admitted. "I'm sorry for it."

"Did ye quarrel?"

Lennox pulled a face. "Something like that."

Davina said nothing else, clearly noting the edge to his voice.

"Sorry," he muttered. "I'm just not used to talking about it."

"Ye don't have to," she assured him.

"No, but ye asked." He paused then, searching for the words to describe his relationship with his elder brother. "Over the years, people have asked me ... yer father included ... if I wished I were the first-born son. But I didn't. I never coveted my brother's position. I've always looked up to Iver ... he was born to rule Dun Ugadale ... but growing up, I felt the odd one out. I've got a quick temper, and I can be reckless, and when Iver took over as laird, he handled me as ye would a hot coal."

Lennox broke off there. He wasn't sure what he was trying to say, only that, now that the words tumbled out of him, he wanted to set everything inside him free. Instinctively, he knew Davina wouldn't judge him. Not after everything she'd been through of late. "I'm the second eldest, yet instead of making me Captain of the Guard as I'd hoped, he gave that role to Kerr, our younger brother ... and made me his bailiff."

"Ye'd make a good bailiff," Davina replied.

He snorted, noting her wry tone. "I'm aggressive, ye mean?"

"I never said that," she teased.

"Aye, well ... I *was* a decent enough bailiff, although arresting criminals and threatening tenants who are overdue on their rents wasn't the life I'd imagined for myself. With the years, I grew increasingly restless ... and when we stopped at Kilchurn on the way home from Stirling, and yer father offered me a position, I decided I'd had enough of pretending to be happy."

Silence fell once more as Davina took in his words. When she replied, her voice was thoughtful. "But ye weren't any happier at Kilchurn, were ye?"

"No" he admitted quietly.

"So, do ye know what ye want now?"

Her question threw him, and he considered it for a few moments before answering. "I wish I could say 'aye', lass," he murmured, "but the past days have thrown everything into upheaval." He grimaced. "I don't think I've ever felt as lost as I do now."

Her grip on his waist tightened just a fraction. In truth, riding double with this woman over the past two days had been a distraction he didn't need. The feel of her slight body against his brought up desires he desperately tried to quash.

Davina was vulnerable, and she needed his help. He wouldn't take advantage of her.

There was nothing sensual in the way she touched him now. Instead, she was trying to reassure him. "This is my doing," she murmured. "I've ruined yer prospects at Kilchurn. I'm sorry, Mackay."

Shifting his left hand, which had been resting on his thigh, for his right one held the reins, he brought it up and placed it over hers. "Don't be," he replied. "I need to go home ... I need to face things."

They stopped to rest around noon, on the bank of a narrow burn in a shallow wooded vale. Clear water bubbled over peaty soil while a pair of goshawks wheeled overhead.

Davina had noticed that the farther south they rode, the wider the sky became. Mackay had told her that they'd reach the edge of the peninsula by nightfall and then strike out onto it the following morning.

Even though her disappointment at being refused entry at Iona still stung, she found herself looking forward to seeing Lennox Mackay's home. It wasn't the sanctuary she'd hoped for, but it would allow her to make a fresh start, all the same. She was fortunate indeed that this man had come to her aid.

How would she ever repay him?

Their noon meal was delicious—nutty bread, butter, and boiled eggs—and Davina ate hungrily.

"Ye look happier than ye did at Kilchurn, lass." She glanced up to see Mackay watching her. "Despite everything that has befallen ye, of late."

Davina shrugged. "I couldn't breathe within those walls." She pulled a face then. "Not after what happened to Blair. Everywhere I turned, there were memories."

Mackay's brow furrowed. "Do ye still miss him?"

Davina stilled. His question surprised her. "It's a year now," she admitted with a sad smile. "And his loss cast a shadow over my days for most of that time. However, now that we are far from Kilchurn, that shadow has drawn back." She paused then. "It's strange, but although this trip has been a disaster, I feel as if a burden has been lifted from my shoulders."

He nodded, his gaze thoughtful. "It sounds as if neither of us belonged at Kilchurn."

Davina shook her head. She popped her last piece of bread into her mouth and brushed the crumbs off her skirts before glancing up at him once more, almost shy this time. She was used to verbally sparring with Lennox Mackay; it felt strange to converse so openly with him.

"Bonnie will be delighted to see ye when we reach Dun Ugadale, I'd wager," Mackay announced then, smoothly changing the subject. "After months defending herself from my mother's barbs, she'll be desperate for gentler company."

Davina laughed. "Yer mother is a woman to be reckoned with then?"

He grinned. "Aye, ye could say that. She—"

The snapping of twigs underfoot cut Mackay off.

Twisting around on the flat rock she'd sat down on to eat, Davina spied figures bursting from a growth of twisted, gnarled willows.

Three men in travel-stained braies, léines, and leather vests, their hair wild and their expressions savage, barreled toward the bank of the burn.

Panic jolted into her, for she recognized them.

They were the three Stewarts they'd faced on the way to Oban—the men Mackay had sent scurrying for the hills.

16: HIS AVENGING ANGEL

MACKAY CURSED BEFORE rolling to his feet with breathtaking speed.

An instant later, he'd drawn his dirk and moved forward to face their attackers. "Get to the horse, Davina, and ride!"

Davina scrambled to her feet, her legs tangling in her skirts as she did so. She didn't bother to pick up the remnants of their meal, or the skin of ale. Instead, she backed off toward where the gelding stood.

Moments earlier, the horse had been cropping at grass, but when the men had exploded from the trees, the beast startled. It snorted nervously as Davina approached.

Meanwhile, Mackay had engaged the warriors.

"Did ye think we'd let ye get away with interfering in the king's business?" One warrior, the biggest of the three, with a bandaged arm, shouted.

Mackay didn't answer. It was a rhetorical question.

"Ye helped a Douglas ... and that makes ye a traitor to the crown," another warrior roared.

Davina's heart lurched into her throat. Three against one. It wasn't going to be a fair fight.

He'd ordered her to ride, but she couldn't let him face them on his own, couldn't just ride off and let them butcher him.

Nonetheless, the man knew how to handle himself in a fight. Once, during the noon meal at Kilchurn, she'd heard her father boasting about how well his new captain wielded a blade. Davina had only half-listened, for she'd been too unhappy to focus on her father's words. However, watching him now, it seemed he was right.

Lennox Mackay was fast and deadly. He didn't hesitate, didn't show any fear of the slashing dirk-blades.

One warrior cut him across the arm, yet he dove under his guard and drove his dirk between the man's ribs, shoving him into the path of his companions.

The man's agonized cry echoed across the wooded valley, and he crumpled.

But the others kept coming.

Jaw clenched, Davina looked frantically around her for a weapon. As a lass, her father had taught her how to defend herself and how to hunt. She wasn't bad with a knife, but she was better with a bow and arrow.

She was out of practice though—it had been years.

Reaching the nervous horse, she quietened the beast with a murmured word and a soothing stroke to its neck. She then grabbed Mackay's bow and quiver from where he'd strapped them to the back of the saddle.

Her hands fumbled as she slung the quiver over her shoulder and grabbed an arrow.

Curse it, she was so nervous she wouldn't be able to shoot straight.

Her gaze cut to where Mackay was circling his two remaining adversaries. The big one was hunched over, his face scrunched up in pain. Mackay had clearly managed to wound him. Yet the man's gaze blazed with fury.

Notching her arrow, Davina moved into position and drew the bowstring taut, sighting her quarry.

And curse it again, they were too close to Mackay at present, dirk-blades flashing in the noon sun. If she tried to shoot one of them, she risked sticking him instead. None of them had noticed her standing there. In a knife fight like this, it was too dangerous to look away, even for an instant.

The arrow trembled as Davina waited.

Her arms weren't strong enough to hold this position for long.

All the same, she wasn't getting up on that horse and galloping to safety. She wasn't leaving Mackay on his own.

He fought with breathtaking skill, yet it was clear the two he dueled with were also seasoned warriors. All three of them were moving dizzyingly fast, ignoring the prostrate figure of the man on the ground.

"Wait, lass," Davina whispered, trying to ignore the thunder of her pulse in her ears and the sweat that now trickled down her back. "They'll circle each other again soon."

She'd watched her father's warriors spar enough times to know how fights played out. It was like observing a treacherous dance. And when her father and Blair had fought with dirks, they'd attacked in bursts before circling each other once more, waiting for their next chance.

The warriors drew apart, their breathing coming in rasping pants now. All three—including Mackay—were bleeding, but now there was space between them.

Davina sighted the big warrior, the most threatening of them all, and loosed her arrow.

Thud.

It hit him in the hollow of the neck.

The Stewart warrior reeled back, his dirk slipping from his fingers as he clutched at the arrow.

But Mackay had already turned his attention from him.

The last of his attackers had been distracted for an instant, and Mackay dived at the man, slamming his blade up through the underside of his jaw.

The warrior collapsed like a sack of barley.

Mackay swiveled back to the warrior Davina had shot. He lay on his back now, his breath a wheezing death rattle as he stared up at the sky. Moments slid by, and then he, like the two others sprawled on the ground nearby, went limp.

Only then did Lennox Mackay turn his attention to Davina.

Breathing hard, his gaze slid over to where she stood, a new arrow readied to fire. His eyes widened. "I thought I told ye to take my horse and ride," he panted.

Davina inclined her head, managing a tight smile despite her galloping heart. "Aye," she gasped, almost as breathless as he was. "It's just as well I never do as I'm told."

They dragged the corpses of the three Stewarts into the trees, covering them with foliage so they wouldn't be seen from the road. In a day or two, they'd start to stink, but by then, Lennox and Davina would be far away.

Returning to where Davina stood next to their skittish gelding, Lennox's gaze lingered on her. She wasn't looking at him; she was too busy soothing the nervous horse. The beast could smell blood and had witnessed the short yet brutal fight. Its nostrils were flared, and it carried its head unnaturally high as if it wished to kick up its heels and bolt at any moment.

Wary, Lennox slowed his gait. Of course, the blood of the men he'd fought was on him. He didn't want the gelding to take off, leaving them to walk the rest of the way to Dun Ugadale.

However, Davina appeared to be doing a fine job of calming the beast. She murmured soft words and gently stroked its trembling neck. Her crooning tone and the tenderness in her voice made him slow his pace further, and his breathing grew shallow.

His gaze shifted from the horse then, taking her in once more.

The forest-green kirtle and matching cloak she wore were both travel-stained, and locks of raven hair had come loose from her tight braid, framing her lovely face.

Lennox's heart kicked against his ribcage.

How had he not found her enchanting at Kilchurn? How had he spent mealtimes in her company without staring at her like a mooncalf? Davina Campbell was an angel—*his* avenging angel.

She'd been brave. Her aim had been excellent and deadly, and the truth be known, he'd needed her assistance. As good as he was with a knife, his adversaries were equally skilled.

Aye, she was as slender as a willow branch, yet her determination and strength belied her fragile appearance. She could be cold and haughty one moment, and emotional and passionate the next. Everything about her was a contradiction. Lennox had never met a woman like her, and he doubted he would again.

"Ye have soothed our mount well, I see," he said, reaching her side.

Indeed, the gelding had now lowered its head, huffing gently when Lennox patted its neck.

Davina glanced up, flashing Lennox a smile that made his already hammering pulse quicken further. "Aye, it feels good to be a help rather than a hindrance, for once," she admitted. "I do believe our steed is ready to bear us south once more."

18: HONORABLE

THEY ENDED THE day in the hamlet of Inverneil.
Perched near the coast, next to a stone bridge spanning a
wide burn, the village was a welcome sight after an
exhausting day. Despite the weariness that pressed down
upon her shoulders, Davina's mouth lifted at the edges
as they approached Gilip Tavern, a squat stacked-stone
establishment with a neatly thatched roof.

"I've stayed here before," Mackay informed her as he
guided the gelding around the back to the adjoining
stables. "Best mutton pies on the west coast of Scotland."

Davina huffed a tired laugh at this proclamation.
"Aye, and have ye tried them all?"

"Enough to judge," he assured her. "It's a welcoming
place too … we'll be well looked after."

This news was a relief indeed. After the skirmish at
noon, Davina's nerves had jangled for the rest of the day.
And even though the men who'd tracked them down
from Oban were all dead, it had been an effort not to
steal anxious glances over her shoulder.

She'd killed someone.

Davina had expected to go to pieces in the aftermath
of shooting an arrow through that warrior's neck, but in
the wake of the attack, a strange calm had settled over
her. She kept waiting for the storm to break, although it
hadn't yet.

Perhaps it would later when she was alone.

"Will ye tell yer brother that we killed the king's
men?" she asked after a pause.

Mackay nodded, his mouth thinning. "He'll understand that we weren't given any choice," he replied. "Although we're fortunate indeed that no one witnessed that fight. The last thing my family needs is the king's wrath."

Davina nodded, even as disquiet feathered through her.

Theirs was the only horse stabled at the tavern this evening, which meant there would be plenty of rooms available inside. Mackay was running low on coin, so Davina paid for two chambers side-by-side at the back, with windows overlooking the hills to the west. She then ordered supper to be brought up for them both and hot baths to be drawn.

Before she retired next door, Davina insisted on looking at the injuries her companion had sustained during the fight. There were three cuts—two to his right arm, and one across his ribs—but luckily, all were shallow. Nonetheless, Davina asked for some vinegar and fresh linen to be brought up to Mackay's chamber. She then tended to him.

"They're just scratches," he muttered, stripping off his soiled and bloodied léine. "There's no need to fash yerself."

Davina harrumphed. "My mother taught me that even the most innocuous-looking scratch can turn sour if not tended well," she told him sternly as she poured vinegar onto a strip of cloth. "And she was a wise woman indeed."

Lennox huffed a long-suffering sigh, seating himself on a stool by the open window. It was a mild evening, and the innkeeper hadn't bothered to light the hearths. The blustery wind had died with the setting sun. "Go on then."

Davina stepped close, her brow furrowing. "Lift yer arm up," she instructed. "I'll see to the cut on yer ribs first." She was careful to keep her focus on his wounds, not on the fact that an attractive man was sitting half-naked in front of her.

Mackay yelped when she placed the vinegar-soaked cloth on the cut, wiping away the crusted blood.

"Christ's bones, woman," he hissed through clenched teeth. "It burns."

Davina snorted. His reaction reminded her of her father's. Colin Campbell wouldn't so much as let out a groan of pain in front of his men after a fight, but when alone with his womenfolk, he whimpered like a bairn.

Thoughts of her father shadowed her mood, sadness tugging at her. She wondered how he'd take the news that she'd lost her dowry and would be residing at Dun Ugadale. Would he care at all?

"Hold still," she said, dabbing at the wound once more. "I want to make sure it's clean."

He flinched, and she muttered a curse under her breath, continuing her ministrations until she was satisfied the wound was properly cleansed. She then drew back and took hold of his right wrist, bringing his arm up so that she could wash the cuts there too. "Ye are fortunate," she murmured, pouring vinegar onto a fresh cloth. "None of these need stitching."

He made a strangled noise in response.

Mouth twitching, for it was hard not to tease him, Davina began dabbing at the wound on his forearm. All the while, she held onto his wrist—and to her surprise, she could feel his pulse fluttering against her fingertips.

Surely, she wasn't causing him that much pain?

When she glanced up, she noticed that he wasn't grimacing any longer. Instead, he was watching her—and the intensity in his eyes made her heart roll over.

It was that same look he'd given her right before they kissed days earlier. A look that made her breathing grow shallow and caused heat to ignite low in her belly.

Such a stare could make a woman forget herself.

Davina ducked her head once more and deftly cleaned the final of the three cuts, on his bicep. Then, still avoiding his eye, she reached for the last of the clean linen, tore off three strips, and bound his wounds carefully.

"Ye will want to have a healer check these injuries once we reach Dun Ugadale," she said briskly. "Just to ensure they haven't festered."

"I shall," he assured her. "Although I'm sure ye have done a fine job, Davina."

Stepping back, her fingers tightening around the clay bottle of vinegar she held, Davina picked up the cork and stoppered it. To her chagrin, she found her hands were shaking just a little. Dizziness swept over her then. Perhaps she should have asked one of the serving lasses to tend to Mackay's injuries. She couldn't trust herself around him. "Aye, well ... let's hope so," she replied.

She lifted her chin then, meeting his gaze once more.

Heat flushed through her when she saw he was smiling, a knowing glint in those midnight-blue eyes. Curse the knave, he knew why she was avoiding his gaze.

"I'll leave ye now then," she said, motioning to the steaming tub of water sitting near the hearth. "A bath also awaits me in my chamber, and I don't want it to get cold."

"Aye." Mackay rose to his feet, his eyes crinkling at the corners as he flashed her another smile, a warm rather than teasing one this time. "Will ye join me for supper later?" He paused then, their gazes fusing. "I must admit, I've never enjoyed eating alone."

Davina took a bite of mutton pie and sighed. Glancing up, she saw Mackay was watching her. Fortunately, it wasn't with that hot gaze of earlier. Instead, his expression was expectant. "What do ye think?"

Davina swallowed her mouthful. "It's delicious."

He winked at her. "I told ye they were good."

Smiling, Davina focused on her supper once more. They sat in companionable silence for a while then, at the table by the window in his chamber. Outdoors, the sky had turned dark-blue—the color of Mackay's eyes—and the shrill notes of a Highland pipe from the common room below drifted up, echoing through the stillness.

"It sounds as if they're having a merry time downstairs," Mackay noted eventually, with a wry smile. He'd nearly finished his pie, while she was only halfway through hers. "Are ye sure ye don't want to join them?"

Davina shook her head. "I've had more than enough excitement for one day," she replied. "I'm happy to sit up here ... and have a little peace."

Below, off-tune, drunken singing accompanied the pipe, and Mackay grimaced. "Aye, well ... that's probably wise."

"Ye can go down, if ye wish?"

Their gazes met, and his mouth curved once more. "No, ye are much better company ... I'd rather stay here."

Davina's heart did a little patter at this. She too had no desire to be anywhere else at present.

Mackay leaned back in his chair then, his fingers wrapping around the tankard of ale. "Ye showed an impressive aim with that bow and arrow today."

Her lips curved. "I wish I could agree with ye, Mackay, but it was a lucky shot. I'm out of practice ... and I was shaking so badly, I'm surprised I could shoot straight all."

He snorted. "Nonsense. Yet hit the man square in the throat." He shook his head then, his expression sobering. "I'm sorry ye had to witness all of that, Davina." Their gazes met and held. "And yet ye are remarkably calm this evening. I expected to see ye more shaken."

She sighed. "I *am* shaken, but I've the wits to realize that some occasions call for violence." She paused then, favoring him with an arch look. "I wasn't going to ride away and leave ye to deal with them alone."

The moment drew out before he smiled and lifted his tankard to his lips.

Davina dropped her gaze to the pie and continued eating. Despite that she was enjoying it, the pie was huge, and she eventually gave up, pushing the dish away.

"Ye aren't going to finish that?" Mackay asked.

She laughed, noting the hungry way he was eyeing her meal—and it struck her then that she hadn't laughed properly in a long while. It felt strange. "No, ye are welcome to though, if ye wish?"

The man didn't need to be asked twice. Pulling her dish close, he tucked in.

Davina watched him eat, a smile tugging at her lips. She then picked up her own tankard, taking a sip. Like the pie, it was a credit to this tavern—cool with the sharp flavor of hops. A sensation of well-being filtered over her then. Maybe it was the good food or her sudden burst of mirth, but for a few instants, she forgot her cares. She didn't ruminate over the past or worry about the future; instead, she just eased into the moment.

The rise and fall of the pipe, accompanied by merry, if raucous, singing and the caress of sweet summer air on her face through the open window made her feel as if there was no other place she'd rather be than here right now.

Like laughter, it was a strange sensation. After Blair's death, she'd spent her days wishing she were somewhere else.

But this evening, she was content.

"I don't think I've thanked ye properly for offering me yer kin's hospitality, Mackay," she said after a lengthy pause. Her companion had just finished his last bite of pie and was washing it down with a mouthful of ale. "Ye must think I lack manners."

He glanced up before shaking his head. "I think ye've had yer mind filled with more important matters," he replied. She was grateful to note there was no teasing edge to his voice now. His face was serious.

"Even so, I want ye to know that yer kindness has not gone unnoticed," she said softly.

His gaze glinted. "My *kindness?*"

"Aye ... ye have acted honorably. I don't know how I shall ever repay ye."

Did she imagine it or did his shoulders stiffen? A moment later, he cut his gaze away. "I couldn't let ye stay on in Oban ... alone," he said, his manner a little stiff now. Davina wondered what was wrong.

"But ye would have, had I insisted?"

He glanced her way again, his gaze narrowing. He then raised his tankard to his lips and took another gulp before replying, "No ... I'd have remained with ye."

It was Davina's turn to tense now, her eyes snapping wide. "Ye would?"

His attention didn't waver from hers. "Aye, I'd have found work there and ensured ye were taken care of."

Her heart jolted against her breastbone. "But why?"

"Ye are a gently bred woman, Davina ... only a heartless turd would leave ye alone in a rough port. There are plenty of unscrupulous sorts who'd prey upon a lady."

He took another sip from his tankard, although his attention remained upon her face.

Davina started to sweat. "Ye'd do that for me?" she asked after a weighty pause.

He held her gaze. Silence swelled between them, tension rippling across the table. "Aye," Mackay replied eventually. "I would."

Mackay's gaze smoldered as their stare drew out. Davina's breathing caught. If she'd been made of wax, she'd have melted under that look. And just like earlier, need slammed into her, making her tremble.

Hades, she had to distance herself from this man before she threw herself at him.

Clearing her throat, Davina pushed herself away from the table and rose to her feet. "I should go," she announced.

Turning, she moved toward the door, yet she was just two feet from it when Lennox's hand closed around her arm, halting her.

Breathing hard, as though she'd just raced up the stairs rather than crossed the chamber, Davina froze to the spot. She didn't turn to him, didn't glance his way.

Instead, she stood there, rigid, her heart pounding.

He stepped closer to her, and the heat of his body caressed her back, even though they weren't touching.

"Ye see, I'm not as *honorable* as ye think, Davina," he whispered hoarsely, his breath feathering across her ear and neck. "A decent man wouldn't entertain impure thoughts about ye. He wouldn't imagine peeling off that pretty kirtle of yers ... but I do. I *burn* to do all manner of wicked things to ye."

Davina stifled a gasp.

Lord, she should be outraged by such an admission. She should tell him that he was the basest of knaves, rip her arm from his hold, and storm from the chamber.

But she wasn't outraged. Quite the opposite.

Indeed, her knees started to shake, desperate hunger twisting low in her belly. Long moments passed, and then, slowly, she turned to him. Lennox released her, yet he didn't move away. Indeed, he was standing so close that she could smell the hint of rosemary and cedar from the soap he'd used to bathe, so close that she was staring straight into the hollow of his throat above his loosely laced léine. His pulse fluttered there.

Exhaling, she raised a hand and placed it upon his chest. The léine he wore was made of thin linen, and she could feel the heat of his skin like a brand against her palm.

Blood roaring in her ears, she then lifted her chin, letting their gazes fuse.

And it was as powerful as before. This close, he drew her in, made everything else disappear. She felt as if she were standing on the edge of a windswept cliff, and all she had to do was lean forward, and she would topple off into a wild, churning sea.

It was as if her life were about to end and begin at the same time. It was dangerous yet thrilling.

She swallowed, wetting her suddenly parched lips with the tip of her tongue. And then, without letting herself think about what she was doing, she went up on tiptoe and brushed her mouth against his.

19: WICKED

HIS LIPS WERE soft and warm, yet firm. Heart hammering, Davina drew back to see his reaction.

Mackay was staring down at her with a look of feral hunger on his face, one that made her already labored breathing quicken further.

She noted then that his chest rose and fell sharply now. Davina stared up at him, her other hand coming up to trace his freshly shaven jaw. "Kiss me, Lennox," she whispered.

That was all it took. With a groan low in his throat, he dipped his head, his mouth claiming hers.

And just like the evening in Oban, when they'd argued and then he'd kissed her, his embrace was fierce. Only this time, Davina didn't draw back and slap him for his impudence. This time, she matched him. Going up on her toes once more, she wrapped her arms around his neck, her mouth feverishly attacking his.

Mackay's hands were on her back now, sliding down her spine. And then, he grasped her backside, hauling her hard against him.

Their bodies were flush, and although they were still fully clothed, Davina felt him: his hard body and the hot, solid length of his erection pressing into her.

Excitement swooped through Davina at this discovery, and without questioning her behavior, she let her hand travel down his torso, sliding it between them to where his shaft twitched against her belly.

She traced its swollen length with her fingertips, marveling at how it grew larger and harder still.

Mackay groaned again, the sound almost a growl.

Tearing his mouth from hers, he stepped back and started undoing the laces at the front of her kirtle. "I need to see ye," he rasped.

Davina plucked at his léine, her fingers then fumbling with the laces of his braies. "And I must see *ye*," she whispered back. "Now."

His lips curved, even as his eyes had hooded with desire. "As ye wish, my lady."

They wrestled out of their clothing, the garments pooling on the scrubbed wooden floor, before falling into each other's arms once more. Mackay's hands were everywhere, as was his hot mouth. It left her lips, trailing down her jaw and throat, to where her breasts ached to be touched.

Panting, she gazed down at him as he drew an engorged nipple into his mouth, teasing it with his tongue before he started to suck.

Davina cried out, writhing against his mouth. Meanwhile, his hands grasped her backside once again, kneading her soft flesh.

"God help me, ye are lovely, Davina," he groaned as he tore his mouth from her aching nipple and changed to her other breast. "Ye taste like cream and honey."

Davina merely muttered something incoherent in reply, arching into him as he suckled her once more. Her whole body ached for his touch now. They still stood by the door, yet her legs wobbled as if she were a newborn foal.

Mackay sucked her nipple hard then, his teeth grazing over it, and her knees buckled. She fell into him, and he scooped her up into his arms, carrying her over to the bed.

"Remember what I said about wanting to do wicked things to ye, lass?" he growled as they stretched out on the coverlet.

Heat pulsed between Davina's thighs at these words. "Aye," she gasped.

"Well, I shall start now ... come here."

He rolled onto his back and then drew her toward him before turning her around and pulling her astride his face. And then, to her shock, he took hold of her hips and lowered them so that her most intimate spot was splayed open for him.

Her choked cry filled the chamber when his tongue found her. "Lennox!"

"Aye, that's it, lass," he growled. "Sit on my face ... grind yerself into me."

Sweat beaded across Davina's body, wild excitement beating through her as she obeyed. Delicious pleasure started to build, to unfurl in her lower belly and between her thighs as his mouth and tongue pleasured her.

Gasping, she sprawled forward, the tips of her breasts grazing his flat belly. His rod reared up to meet her, and she eagerly wrapped her fingers around its base before she slid its engorged tip in her mouth.

His shaft jerked when she took him deep, and she squirmed against his questing mouth as he increased his ministrations.

The saints forgive her, this *was* wicked indeed. Wicked and thrilling. The way he was touching her, how his tongue darted. It drew her closer to the edge, and she writhed while pleasure steadily built, coiling tighter and tighter with each heartbeat.

She went wild, sucking on his rod hungrily, sliding her mouth up and down his length and taking him so deep that she almost choked, while she stroked his heavy bollocks.

He jerked and bucked against her, even as his mouth didn't cease its exquisite torture.

The building pleasure in Davina's loins exploded then, and wave after wave of melting ecstasy broke over her. She cried out, the sound choked off by his rigid rod lodged deep inside her throat.

Her jaw was starting to ache now, but she didn't stop working him, and an instant later, he arched up off the bed and spilled inside her mouth.

Davina drank him down eagerly, her peak extending as she swallowed the last of his seed.

And then they both collapsed on the bed, exhausted and out of breath.

Heart pounding, Davina wriggled off Mackay. She was aware she was sitting on his face and didn't want to smother the man. Wordlessly, he reached down, drawing her up so that she lay against his flank, their sweat-slicked bodies melded together. Davina rested her heated cheek upon his heaving chest, her hand spread across his thundering heart.

They lay like that for a while, neither of them speaking.

In truth, the power of speech had deserted Davina.

She had no idea couples did things like that together. They hadn't even tumbled, and he'd already transported her to the stars.

And as she lay there, and her racing pulse calmed, she remembered Blair.

Sadness tugged deep in her chest, yet she didn't shy away from the memories. Instead, she let herself relive their time together. After dancing around each other for nearly three years, their affair had been brief and passionate. He'd only taken her twice before that fateful day, and both times had been stolen moments, away from the prying eyes of servants. There hadn't been time to disrobe, to enjoy each other properly. Both times, he'd taken her up against a wall.

She'd never had the opportunity to lie with Blair like this, to let her gaze feast upon his naked body. She'd never taken his shaft in her mouth either or enjoyed him pleasuring her like Mackay just had.

Sorrow flowed through her like a river, and she let it.

"Ye are deep in thought," Mackay said softly after a long while.

Davina stiffened against him, surprised at how perceptive he was. "Aye," she whispered. "Is it that obvious?"

"Aye ... yer breathing has gone shallow." He paused then. "What are ye thinking about?"

"The past."

His fingertips trailed down her spine, caressing her lazily. His touch made a restless ache rise once more between her thighs. Lord, she wasn't yet sated; she still wanted him.

"I know there's no changing what has gone before," she said, deliberately keeping her cheek pressed to his chest. She didn't want to look into his eyes right now, not while she talked about this. "But I blame myself nonetheless." An ache rose under her breastbone then. "As ye have seen, I have an impulsive nature ... and it's forever getting me into trouble."

Mackay didn't reply immediately. And when he did, his voice was even, measured, as if he had thought his answer over carefully. "Ye *do* have a passionate nature, lass ... but that's nothing to be ashamed of."

She sucked in a deep breath. "It is when it ends with death."

"That wasn't yer fault. Yer father wielded the blade that killed yer lover ... not ye."

She hadn't mentioned the incident, yet Lennox was no fool; he knew whom she was talking about.

"Aye, but if I hadn't embarked on that affair so rashly, Blair might be alive now."

He gave a soft snort. "My father once told me that ye should never regret anything that is done with a sincere heart. There was no malice in yer choice, no guile."

Davina fell silent, digesting his words. "Yer father sounds like a wise man."

"He was." She caught the edge to his voice then. "And taken too soon." He paused, his eyes shadowing. "However, he also made a few mistakes ... and one of them was marrying my mother."

Davina's breathing caught, and she lifted her head, her gaze meeting his. "That's quite a claim. Ye should be grateful he did, Lennox Mackay, or ye wouldn't be here."

His mouth lifted at the corners, although his blue eyes remained somber. "It might sound harsh, but ye didn't have to grow up listening to them fight. It shouldn't have been a surprise to anyone when Da found solace in the cook's bed ... but those were stormy times indeed within the broch." He sighed then. "My youngest brother, Brodie, is a result of my father's dalliance though ... so some good came of it." His fingertips continued their sensual path up and down her spine then, his gaze holding hers. "Not every mistake we make ends in tragedy, Davina."

"And what about this?" she breathed.

He inclined his head. "Do ye believe this to be a *mistake*?"

20: A GALLANT OFFER

DAVINA'S BREATHING QUICKENED, and she was suddenly acutely aware of their nakedness, of how her breasts pressed up against his ribs, and the way her leg curled around his calf. "No," she admitted after a moment. "But we might come to regret it later."

"We don't have to go any further, ye know?"

Davina's pulse accelerated, disappointment twisting in her breast. Truth was, she still ached for Lennox and hadn't yet had her fill of him. This evening had just begun; she didn't want it to end so soon.

But he was opening the door for her, letting her choose whether to depart.

His expression was veiled now, his body still as he waited for her response.

"I know," she replied finally. Her hand slid across his chest, across the hard nubs of his nipples. "But perhaps yer father is right ... about regrets. Being here with ye doesn't feel wrong." She halted, her gaze holding his. "I'm three and twenty, and already I have far too many regrets behind me." Davina paused once more, considering her words, before continuing. "But *this* won't be one of them. I promise ye that."

"Yet if we continue, ye may end up carrying my bairn," he said then, his voice roughening. "I don't like to have to point this out, lass ... for I'm nearly crawling out of my skin for wanting ye ... yet I feel I must."

Davina's mouth quirked. "And ye tell me ye aren't honorable." She sighed then. "My courses ended just two days ago ... and the healer from the village near Kilchurn once told me that the days just before a woman's moon bleed, during, and just after are relatively safe. If we lie together tonight, it's likely my womb won't quicken."

His eyes widened. "A healer told ye that?"

"Aye."

He snorted. "Sounds like witchcraft to me."

Davina laughed. "No, it's just knowledge." She didn't add that the same healer had told her how to make a draft of herbs, of which the main ingredient was pennyroyal. If a woman took them early enough in her pregnancy, her courses would arrive. She'd made the drink after the first time she and Blair had coupled and could make it again, if necessary. But it wasn't something she wished to share with Mackay. Men tended to take a dim view of such things.

"I understand the risks we're taking," she continued, holding his eye. "And if I were a more sensible woman, I'd get up and leave." Her lips curved into a rueful smile then. "Yet I've never been sensible ... so why start now?"

He laughed, the warm sound rumbling through his chest. And the way he was looking at her, the limpid depths of his eyes, made her stomach do a wild dance.

Aye, he wanted her, and she wanted him—and they'd finish what they started.

Her hand strayed lower, traveling across his belly, and then her breathing hitched when the silky head of his shaft nudged her fingers.

She glanced down then to where his magnificent erection strained toward her.

Davina's breathing hitched, and she was reaching for it when he caught hold of her wrist. "Not this time, lass," he said, his voice breathless now. "This time, I want ye riding my rod, with those pretty tits bouncing in my face."

Dizziness barreled into Davina. Mother Mary, the man had a mouth on him. And the Virgin forgive her, she was no better than him; she loved every filthy thing he said.

Wordlessly, she pushed herself up and straddled him. Placing the head of his shaft at her entrance, she slowly sank down on him. And as she did so, her gaze never left his.

Mackay's lips parted while she slid down his engorged length. She took him in to the hilt, settling against him so their bodies were flush. And then she rolled her hips.

The sensation was so delicious that Davina let out a low, needy groan.

Mackay moaned her name and gripped her hips. She then began to rock, sliding up and down his shaft in smooth, slow movements.

It didn't take long before excitement quickened in her loins. Sweat beaded over her body. Wildness ignited. And suddenly, she forgot herself. Indeed, she did ride Mackay—hard—writhing and moaning each time she impaled herself on him.

She was vaguely aware of her lover's groans joining hers. His fingers tightened on her hips, slamming her down on him now. She watched his face—the flush upon his high cheekbones and the way his eyes glittered with lust.

The intensity of their gazes meeting was too much. Pleasure twisted deep in her womb, rippling out in powerful, aching pulses—and Davina shattered.

Arching, she threw her head back, her raw cry blending with the shrill wail of the Highland pipe that serenaded them.

They fell asleep in each other's arms.

Lennox hadn't meant to drift off. However, the torpor that rolled over him after his release was so powerful that he couldn't resist it. He fell into a deep, peaceful slumber.

He was usually a light and fitful sleeper, yet tonight he didn't wake in the early hours of the morning as was his habit—staring up at the rafters and wishing it were dawn already. On this occasion, he awoke to the morning light caressing his face, streaming in through the open window.

Outside, a rooster was crowing.

Stretching languorously, he became aware that he wasn't alone in the bed.

Soft hair that smelled of lavender tickled his nose, and he glanced down to find a slender figure curled against him.

Davina's face was snuggled into the hollow of his shoulder, and her breathing was slow and deep.

She was still asleep, so Lennox took the opportunity to observe her. She was lovely, her pale skin gleaming like polished marble in the morning light, her silky hair cascading over his chest, as black as raven feathers. She had long, coltish limbs and delicate bones. Aye, she was thin, yet there was nothing fragile about her.

He'd never lain with a woman like Davina. She'd shattered all his preconceived notions about what he wanted in a lover, what attracted him.

Davina Campbell had given him a night quite unlike any other.

She was insatiable—although so was he.

They'd coupled twice more, their bodies slick with sweat, the rasp of their labored breathing filling the bedchamber. He'd taken her first on her hands and knees, thrusting into her from behind, and then on her back, those long legs hooked over his shoulders.

And Davina had met him, thrust for thrust, while she whispered words of encouragement and pleas for him to take her harder, deeper.

Lennox's breathing grew shallow at the memory, his pulse jumping in the hollow of his throat. It had been unforgettable.

But now, daylight filtered in through the window, and the sounds of industry—the clip-clop of horses' hooves on the road and the rumble of men's voices—drifted in, reminding him that the moments he wanted to keep ahold of always passed too quickly.

Reaching across, he gently brushed Davina's hair aside so he could see her face. Her dark lashes lay against her pale cheeks. In sleep, she looked angelic. It was her eyes that betrayed her. They were filled with keen intelligence and a fire that made it difficult for him to look away whenever their gazes locked.

He stroked her smooth cheek, and Davina stirred, her eyelashes fluttering as her eyes opened.

"It's well after dawn, lass," he murmured. "I suppose we shouldn't lie abed."

She yawned, stretching that lissome body against him. "I don't think I've ever slept so well," she admitted huskily.

"Nor I."

Their gazes met, and Lennox's belly tightened. The devil take him, he didn't want to leave this chamber for another two days. Instead, he wanted to remain in bed with Davina and swive her until they both collapsed from exhaustion.

"I enjoyed last night, Lennox," she whispered then, a pretty blush rising to her cheeks.

His lips curved. He liked the soft and sensual way she said his christian name. "I'm relieved to hear it," he replied.

But even as he answered, tension curled under his ribcage. Although they hadn't said as much, they both knew their night together couldn't be repeated. They were alone here, away from the prying eyes of kin. But they couldn't be creeping into each other's beds at Dun Ugadale. His brother would frown upon such behavior.

Lennox cleared his throat. "I would like to make sure ye are safe in the future, Davina, cared for."

She rolled over, propping herself up on an elbow as she regarded him. "Aye, and from what ye have told me, Dun Ugadale will provide that haven."

Lennox drew in a deep breath, even as his stomach clenched.

Cods, he was *never* nervous around women. But with Davina, it was different. She got under his skin. She made him consider things he'd previously ignored.

The idea that one day he might take a wife.

"My brother's broch will provide a haven, aye," he continued, wishing his voice was more insouciant. "But ye will still be a woman alone." He paused then as his pulse tripled. "If I was to take ye as my wife, ye would be under my protection."

Her grey-blue eyes snapped wide, her expression stilling.

Her reaction unsettled him. "I would treat ye well," he assured her quickly. "And although I'm no longer my brother's bailiff, I shall find another role soon enough. Ye would be well looked after."

Davina stared back at him before, eventually, her mouth tugged into a wry smile. "Och, Lennox. Ye have already helped me too much ... I can't ask anything else of ye. Yer offer is gallant, yet I will not ask ye to shackle yerself to me."

His already fast pulse started to hammer. "I wouldn't be shackled to ye, I—"

"Hush." Her hand rose, her warm fingers pressing against his lips. "I made a vow I would never wed, and I intend to keep it."

He stiffened, and she removed her hand. "But that was when ye intended to become a nun. Things are different now."

Her expression grew serious, and she swallowed, her slender throat bobbing. "Aye ... but my feelings haven't changed."

He frowned. He didn't understand—she'd already admitted to him she wasn't pious. "Why?"

Her gaze never wavered. "I'm trouble, Lennox ... even my own father washed his hands of me. I don't think I'm meant to be a wife. There are plenty of ways for me to live a fulfilled life. I intend to make myself indispensable at Dun Ugadale ... to be a burden to no one. It's the least I can do."

"But don't ye want bairns ... a husband to grow old with?" Even as Lennox said these words, a queasy sensation rippled through him. He was pushing things, yet he couldn't help it. He didn't understand why she was being so obstinate.

Her face tensed, her eyes hardening slightly. "I did once ... before life taught me some harsh lessons. I'm sorry, Lennox, but I can't marry ye."

Their gazes held, and Lennox suppressed a wince. Her refusal stung, yet he'd accept it.

"Very well," he said, eventually breaking the awkward silence between them. "Ye are right ... it's a foolish idea indeed. Forget I said anything."

21: CONSEQUENCES

DAVINA GLANCED UP, her gaze following a diving swallow. The sky was a pale-blue from one horizon to another this morning, and the air was sweet with the smell of grass—yet also contained the salty tang of the sea. They'd left Inverneil far behind now, traveling south upon a dirt road that hugged the coast.

The sun was on her back, and thistles waved in the breeze upon the surrounding hills.

After the wonderful night she'd just spent with Lennox, Davina's muscles were loose. However, their conversation at dawn had put her on edge. She couldn't believe he'd proposed to her. What was the man thinking?

They'd gotten up shortly after, washed, and dressed, before going downstairs to break their fast with fresh bannocks, butter, and heather honey. They'd said little as they ate and set out shortly after. It was reaching noon now, and they'd barely exchanged two words since their departure from Inverneil.

Lennox had been polite toward her, and considerate, but there was a tension between them that hadn't been there before.

Davina's brow furrowed.

She was to blame.

She hadn't wanted to hurt his feelings, for his offer was kind. Lennox surprised her. Just days earlier, she'd have sworn he wouldn't put himself out for anyone unless there was something in it for him. But she'd misjudged him. Lennox was far more honorable than she'd realized.

Yet this morning, he'd unwittingly crossed a line.

Like most men, he thought that by taking control of her destiny, he was helping her. On the contrary, he wasn't. And despite that she'd tried to explain her motivations to him, she wasn't sure he understood why she wished to remain unwed.

Nonetheless, the rift between them—especially after what they'd recently shared—upset her. She'd thought he'd be the sort to bed a lass and then let her go. He hadn't seemed the kind of man to try and take responsibility afterward. And yet, he'd proposed.

I did him a favor by refusing, she told herself. *When Lennox takes a wife, it should be to a sweet, easy-tempered lass, not a troublesome, disgraced lady.* Like her, he could be reckless. But had she accepted his offer, he'd have regretted it.

Nonetheless, the thought of Lennox taking another woman to his bed, of him looking at anyone else the way he did at her, made her stomach twist. Shoving her ridiculous jealousy aside, Davina cleared her throat, breaking the brittle silence between them. "I have offended ye, haven't I?"

Like the previous days, she was seated behind him. As such, Davina couldn't see his face. Even so, she felt the tension in his back.

Lennox huffed a laugh. "No."

"I'm sorry ... I was blunter than I intended. My father has always despaired of my plain speech."

"I like it," he replied.

"Do ye? That must be why we constantly tangle horns."

He gave a soft laugh. "I like that too." The admission made warmth steal across her chest. He did? "Ye know yer own mind ... and aren't afraid to speak it. There is something admirable in that."

Davina didn't know what to say to such a comment.

Not for the first time, the man took her aback. She'd expected him to be sore about her rejection, and she did sense his hurt, yet he was determined not to let it show. His decency made guilt constrict her chest.

As if sensing her inner turmoil, he shifted his hand to where one of hers loosely held onto his waist. He then squeezed gently. "Fear not, lass ... I'm not offended."

"The Mackays are having problems with their tenants again," a merchant at the next table told his drinking companions. "They're fighting amongst themselves ... and poaching each other's livestock too."

"Iver Mackay won't stand for that," another man rumbled.

Davina tensed, glancing over at Lennox. They were eating supper together downstairs in the busy common room, squeezed in next to fishermen and merchants.

"No, although ye know as well as I, Duncan, that ye can't stop feuding clans so easily," the merchant replied. "It's a pity for Mackay that both the MacAlisters and the MacDonalds dwell upon his lands ... for they hate each other."

Davina noted that Lennox had gone still, his brow furrowed.

After another long day on the road, they'd stopped at the tiny fishing hamlet of Claonaig. The road had brought them south, down the peninsula, before taking them inland for a spell. Then, they'd headed southeast once more. And as they stabled their horse behind a guesthouse near the quay, Lennox had assured Davina they would reach Dun Ugadale the following afternoon at the latest.

She'd met this news with mixed feelings. Relief, for it was wise that she and Lennox didn't prolong their time alone together, and disappointment—for the days she'd spent with him had unfurled something within her. She felt like a flower after a long period of grey skies and rain, turning its face to the sun once more.

Lennox had made her smile again.

They'd been enjoying a delicious meal together too, until talk of problems farther south began at the next table.

The conversation between the other patrons shifted then, while Davina leaned close to Lennox. "Did ye know there was unrest?" she murmured.

His mouth thinned. "The MacAlisters and the MacDonalds have long caused trouble on our lands," he admitted. "But my father managed to end their quarreling." He paused then, heaving a sigh. "However, over the past years, Iver paid little attention to the goings-on around him, and the old arguments have resurfaced. This news comes as little surprise to me."

Davina watched Lennox, noting the lines of tension that now bracketed his mouth. "Ye are worried about seeing yer brother again ... aren't ye?"

Lennox pulled a face before leaning back on his chair and cupping his fingers about the tankard of ale before him. "Not *worried* exactly ... more like wary. As I told ye, we didn't part on the best of terms."

"Ye think he'll humble ye?"

Lennox snorted. "Who knows?" His gaze held hers across the table. "But I'll weather whatever humiliation he serves me ... if it means ye are given a home."

Their stare drew out for a few moments before Davina eventually broke it. Looking down at her half-finished bowl of fish stew, she hurriedly composed herself. "I don't want ye punished because of me," she said quietly.

"Don't worry, Iver won't be harsh," he replied. She glanced up to see him still watching her. His gaze was veiled, although a wry smile played upon his lips. "He'll just enjoy being proved right."

She inclined her head. "About what?"

"That Dun Ugadale is where I belong."

They finished their suppers shortly after that and retired to their separate chambers. Davina didn't venture into Lennox's room this evening, and to her relief, he didn't invite her.

Part of her longed to follow him inside, to close the door on the rest of the world. That foolish part of her wanted to throw herself into his arms, to seek his hungry mouth, and lose herself in him. But the pull she felt toward this man would only get her in trouble. Their conversation at dawn had made that clear enough.

No, the wise thing to do was to avoid lying with him again.

Even so, a hollow sensation settled in her belly when she stepped into her small chamber and listened to the 'thud' of his door closing opposite. Her chamber seemed empty without his company. She already missed the low timbre of his voice, the masculine warmth of his presence.

Goose. Walking across to the nightstand, Davina started to undress. She then poured water from a jug into a wash bowl and went through her ablutions. *Haven't ye learned by now that every action has a consequence?*

The night before, both of them had thrown caution aside. But their conversation in the morning had warned her she needed to be more careful. She needed to look out for herself.

Nervousness tightened Davina's throat then.

Tomorrow they would reach Dun Ugadale, and if Lennox's brother discovered that they'd been lovers, he might force them to wed. She couldn't let that happen.

She would speak to Lennox on the morrow and ensure he would keep their secret.

They were cantering across rolling, windswept hills, north of Dun Ugadale, when Lennox spied horses, riders bent low over their necks, streaming over the ridge ahead. There were around half a dozen of them, fleeing as if the devil himself, with a fiery pitchfork, were after them.

Drawing up his gelding, he squinted at the horizon. His gaze was sharp, yet they were too far away for him to make out their identities. Nonetheless, judging from the horses' flat gallop, they were in a great hurry.

And as he watched, another group of riders appeared over the brow of the hill.

They were giving chase.

"Trouble?" Davina was peering around him and had seen the riders.

Lennox grunted. "Looks like it ... hold on." With that, he gathered the reins and urged his horse into a canter, turning it after the two parties. He wasn't sure what was afoot, but this close to Dun Ugadale, it would involve the Mackays.

He had to know what had happened.

They followed them toward the coast, the gelding's heavy hooves churning up the turf behind it. Davina clung lightly to his waist, keeping her seat easily. As the hills smoothed and Lennox spied Kilbrannan Sound glittering in the distance, he saw that the second group of riders had caught up with the first.

And as he'd suspected, there was trouble—for both groups of men had leaped down from their horses and were now fighting each other.

Lennox slowed his gelding, his gaze sweeping over the skirmish.

Warriors clad in leather, with pine green and dark-blue plaid sashes across their fronts, bore down on men dressed in braies and sweat-stained léines. All the men wielded dirks, although the warriors wearing sashes fought with more skill. One of them, a tall man with shaggy white-blond hair that fell to his shoulders, was clearly in charge. His shouts rang across the hillside as he rallied his men.

Drawing up his horse, Lennox watched from a safe distance.

"Who are they?" Davina asked, her voice tight.

"The Dun Ugadale Guard," he replied. "Dealing with rustlers, I'd wager."

"What should we do?"

"Nothing, lass ... the guard has things in hand."

Indeed, they did, for as he finished speaking, the skirmish ended.

One of the men they'd pursued lay dead on the ground, while the others, most of them bloodied, had thrown aside their dirks and dropped to their knees. The blond warrior pointed the tip of his dirk at the throat of one of them and appeared to be speaking to him.

Satisfied he wasn't going to ride into a melee, Lennox urged his horse forward. And as he drew closer, the leader of the guard spoke. "Did ye think ye would get away with it, MacAlister?"

"I was only taking what was mine." Despite that he had a blade held to his throat, the individual, a huge man with short brown hair and a pugnacious face, didn't cower as some of his companions did. "Ye shouldn't interfere in our business."

"This is *Mackay* land," the blond man replied, his voice cold. "Therefore, it is our business. Ye were warned before, and ye knew what the punishment would be if we ever caught ye thieving livestock again."

The big man's belligerent expression slipped just a little, his face paling beneath his deep tan.

"Last time ye were whipped ... but this time, ye shall lose a hand." The captain's cool gaze shifted to the other rustlers they'd subdued. "*All* of ye shall."

To their credit, none of the men uttered a sound. Nonetheless, Lennox marked how their gazes widened, the whites of their eyes gleaming in the late afternoon sun.

"Ye don't decide that," the first man spluttered. "The laird does."

"Aye, well, let's get ye back to Dun Ugadale, so Iver Mackay can wield the ax himself."

Lennox cleared his throat. "Not bandying words as usual, I see, Kerr."

His brother's broad shoulders tensed. Stepping sideways, his dirk still trained on the rustler, he turned his attention upon where Lennox sat astride his horse, Davina silent behind him.

A heartbeat passed, and then Kerr Mackay's stern face split into a wide grin. "Lennox!"

22: HIGHLAND JUSTICE

"IT'S GOOD TO see ye, brother ... Dun Ugadale hasn't been the same since ye left," Kerr Mackay said quietly.

Although she was still seated behind Lennox, Davina sensed his smile. "Aye, no doubt things here have been dull without me around."

Riding alongside him, Kerr's mouth lifted at the corners. He'd flashed Lennox a wide grin earlier, upon recognizing him, yet his handsome face had returned to its former serious expression now. He appeared to be a man who gave up his smiles grudgingly.

Feeling her gaze upon him, Kerr glanced at Davina. "I'm sorry ye had to see that, Lady Davina," he muttered. "It was a nasty scene ... but unfortunately, there have been many of them, of late."

"Don't mind me," she replied. "I've witnessed worse."

Kerr's blue eyes, similar to Lennox's, although perhaps a shade or two lighter, widened.

"Aye, it's been an eventful ride south," Lennox admitted with a sigh. "And I shall tell ye all once we get home."

Davina's gaze shifted beyond his shoulder to where the high dark-grey walls of Dun Ugadale rose against a cornflower-blue sky. *Home* was before them now.

Her pulse quickened at the sight of the broch and the weathered walls, encrusted with lichen and moss, that wrapped around it. Dun Ugadale looked ancient, as if part of it had been built by those who'd lived here long before the Mackays. A hamlet lay below the broch, small stone bothies nestled amongst the patchwork of tilled fields, and the peaked roof of a kirk speared the sky.

Davina's mouth curved. During the journey south, Lennox had told her of his home. He'd been a little embarrassed, as if worried she'd find it humble in comparison to Kilchurn Castle—but she didn't. Aye, it was considerably smaller, but there was something welcoming about it.

"I can tell there is quite a tale behind yer sudden appearance," Kerr said, eyeing his brother once more. "Ye haven't brought trouble our way, have ye?"

Davina stiffened. She knew he likely wasn't referring to her, and yet guilt constricted her chest. She hoped Kerr's words weren't prophetic.

They inched closer to the causeway that led up to the gates, the road wending through fields where cottars stopped work to gawk at them. Of course, it wasn't Lennox and Davina that drew their attention but the men who walked, hands bound in front of them, at the rear of the Dun Ugadale Guards.

The muttering started, and the cottars exchanged glances. Some of their responses appeared gloating while others were panicked. It occurred to Davina that even in this village, outside the walls of the broch, loyalties were divided.

Tension rippled through the warm afternoon air.

They'd almost reached the causeway when a young woman approached them. She'd sprinted along the path wending between the fields, holding her skirts up to keep from tripping, her curly brown hair flying behind her.

"Da!" she shouted. "What have ye done!"

Davina twisted in the saddle to see the big, belligerent man stumble, his heavy brow furrowing. "Get back, lass."

Ignoring him, she closed the distance between them. Meanwhile, Kerr and his men drew up their horses, watching her approach.

Breathing hard, the woman came to a halt on the roadside. Even from a few yards distant, Davina could see that she was incensed. Her pine-green eyes burned, and a nerve jumped in her cheek. She was tall and well-built, and her impressive bosom heaved as she glared at her father.

MacAlister remained mutinously silent. Frowning, the young woman shifted her ire upon the Captain of the Guard. "If my father won't tell me what he's done, ye must."

Kerr stared her down, his jaw tightening. "He was caught cattle rustling ... again."

Her spine snapped straight, and she put her hands on her hips. "I don't believe ye."

"I'm sorry, Rose, but we caught him and his friends red-handed this time."

The lass scowled at Kerr before her gaze cut to her father. "Why?" she gasped.

"Stay out of this," MacAlister growled. "If ye want to make yerself useful, return home and tell yer brothers what has happened."

She glared back at him, still standing her ground. "Where are they taking ye?"

"Before the chieftain," Kerr replied, his tone inscrutable. "He will decide what their punishment will be."

"He'll take off their right hands!" One of the farmers in the field behind her called out. "And about time too ... I told ye this day would come, Graham MacAlister! That'll teach ye to steal my cousin's cattle."

"Shut yer gob, Aonghus!" MacAlister bawled back, spittle flying. "They were grazing on my turf ... and that makes them—"

"It's not *yer* turf," Kerr interrupted him, his tone icy. "Ye are a tenant on Mackay land, MacAlister. Ye clearly need reminding of some facts."

"Don't ye touch him!" Rose MacAlister stepped forward, her face flushed, her eyes glittering.

"Or what?" Aonghus jeered from behind her. "Ye shall put a curse upon him ... ye aren't taking after yer witchy aunt, are ye?"

Some of the cottars working in the field behind them guffawed at this.

The lass's cheeks flushed red. Yet she ignored the heckling. Her gaze fused with Kerr's, yet neither of them backed down. "Yer father's fate isn't up to me," he said finally, his tone brusque. Kerr then nodded to the other guards. "Let's go."

They rode up the causeway and into the broch, under the iron maw of the portcullis.

And as they went, Rose's angry voice followed them. Her shouts turned to pleas when they stopped inside the barmkin. Watching her, Davina's belly clenched. The lass was desperate now, tears glittering in her green eyes; Davina wished she could help.

"Take Rose back to her brothers," Kerr instructed two of his men gruffly. "She doesn't need to see this."

"No!" The young woman tried to duck away as the husky warriors closed in on her. Yet they cornered her easily, each taking an arm and towing her toward the gate. Rose's cries echoed off stone as they departed.

A heavy silence followed. Not even the clang of iron from the smith's forge shattered it, for the blacksmith himself—a tall man with short brown hair and a scowling face—had emerged to see what the fuss was about.

His gaze swept the crowd before it alighted on Lennox. In an instant, his expression changed. "Len!"

Lennox threw his leg over the front of his saddle and slid lightly down onto the ground. A couple of strides brought the two men together, and they hugged.

Warmth filtered over Davina as she realized this must be Brodie—the youngest of the Mackay brothers, the one who didn't share the same mother.

"I don't believe it." Another male voice boomed across the barmkin, and Davina's gaze cut to where a tall man with long white-blond hair stood on the steps, a red-haired beauty by his side. "Ye've come home."

Iver Mackay was grinning.

Drawing back from Brodie, Lennox turned to face the laird of Dun Ugadale. His mouth quirked, even if his gaze remained wary. "Aye, brother. Am I welcome?"

Iver's smile faded, and he made his way down the steps toward Lennox. He approached him, halting when they stood just a few yards apart. "Didn't I tell ye that ye'd always have a home here?"

"Aye," Lennox replied, "but the passing of the months can change a man's mind."

Their gazes met and held, and then Iver's mouth curved once more. "Well, my words still stand. It's good to see ye, Len."

"And ye," Lennox answered, his voice roughening slightly.

The Mackay chieftain's gaze shifted then, settling upon where Davina still perched in the saddle. "Lady Davina," he greeted her before favoring her with a respectful nod. "What brings ye to Dun Ugadale?"

Davina sucked in a deep breath, readying herself to answer. Lennox beat her to it.

"The lady has fallen upon difficult times, brother ... and wishes to receive sanctuary within these walls." He halted then, waiting as Iver focused on him once more. "I told her that ye would give her what she seeks."

Iver's brow furrowed, his gaze flicking between Lennox and Davina.

Davina's stomach had now tied itself in knots. Although she understood why Lennox had spoken on her behalf, she was irritated he hadn't let her make the request. Nonetheless, the look on the laird's face didn't bode well.

"We shall speak further indoors," Iver said eventually. "For the moment, why don't ye hand yer horse over to one of the lads, and retire to my solar ... I shall join ye shortly." His attention slid away then, to the group of men standing behind them, hands bound, and then to Kerr. His gaze hardened. "Ye found them then?"

Kerr nodded. "Graham MacAlister is their leader."

Iver's brows drew together as he focused on the glowering farmer. He then huffed a deep, weary sigh. "Ye recall what I said to ye the last time, Graham?" he asked, his voice filtering over the silent barmkin.

MacAlister's thick lips flattened, and he gave a jerky nod.

The hardness in the laird's eyes spread to the rest of his face. He then glanced over at Davina. "I invite ye to go inside, Lady Davina ... Bonnie will escort ye."

Realizing that the scene was about to get ugly, Davina nodded.

Lennox stepped forward then, helping her down from the saddle. However, he didn't join her as she walked toward the steps where Bonnie Mackay waited. Iver's wife flashed her a warm smile, even if her sea-green eyes were troubled.

Queasiness rolled over Davina as she imagined what would happen once she and Bonnie had departed.

Justice in the Highlands could be swift and harsh—she'd seen her father deal with thieves in the past.

It wasn't a scene she needed to witness again.

Instead, she focused on the woman she hadn't seen for over five months.

Bonnie had blossomed in her new life. She stood taller, prouder, her fiery hair tamed into an elaborate braid that hung between her shoulder blades. She wore a fine emerald-green surcote with a pea-green kirtle underneath.

The women's gazes met, and Bonnie's mouth tugged into a warm smile. Davina smiled back, the cares that dogged her steps momentarily lifting. Aye, it was good to see Bonnie again.

Lady Mackay held out an arm to her. Gratefully, Davina took it, and together, they walked into the broch.

23: I WILL NOT BE A BURDEN

NO ONE SPOKE when Davina finished her tale.

Those present in the solar had watched her closely as she explained what had befallen her over the past few days. Among them was Sheena—mother to Iver, Lennox, and Kerr. The woman, tall and regal, her white hair braided and wrapped around the crown of her head, had a piercing gaze that Davina wagered missed little.

Davina tried to keep her explanation brief. The only thing she left out was what had happened between her and Lennox—no one needed to hear about that.

The silence that followed her story made Davina nervous. What happened now would decide her future. Her fate was in the laird of Dun Ugadale's hands. Eventually, Iver spoke up. "Yer father won't be pleased when he hears about this."

Davina's throat tightened, her pulse quickening. "He washed his hands of me," she reminded him. "He won't care where I go, or what I do."

The look on the laird's face told her he disagreed. Moments passed, and no one spoke. Lennox looked as if he wished to say something, if the flexing muscle in his jaw was any indication. Yet he held his tongue.

Davina was grateful. She'd told Mackay everything; the decision was now his.

But as she waited, a lump of ice settled in her belly.

If he refused to let her stay, she was in deep trouble. Where would she go? She drew in a deep, steadying breath, trying to quell the panic that fluttered up within. Lennox had told her that the nearest town was Ceann Locha, a busy port south of Dun Ugadale.

She'd have to go there and see if she could find work.

"Yer father is bull-headed," Iver said finally. "But he only let ye go because he thought ye were to live in seclusion upon Iona. When his men return and tell him what has happened, he will have something to say about ye taking refuge here."

"I remember Colin Campbell as a prideful man," Sheena piped up. "I'd wager he will be vexed indeed."

Davina's heart started to pound. She then shared a glance with Lennox. His jaw was clenched now, his brows knitted together. This wasn't how either of them had expected things to go.

Davina's breathing grew shallow. She had to make Lennox's brother understand the gravity of her situation. "He won't," she whispered. "He has disowned me."

The chieftain sighed then, raking a hand through his hair. "I doubt he will forget ye as easily as ye believe, Davina ... yet I will not deny ye sanctuary," he assured her. "Ye may reside at Dun Ugadale."

Davina's breathing caught, relief slamming into her. He didn't appear overjoyed about it, yet the laird was letting her stay, after all.

Iver glanced then at where Bonnie sat by the flickering hearth, his expression softening. "My wife will enjoy yer companionship, and she could do with yer assistance in managing things within the broch."

A warm smile flowered across Bonnie's lovely face. "I could," she agreed.

"Aye, there's always work to be done here," Sheena said then. She was watching Davina with a speculative look, as if assessing whether she was up to the task. "Ye won't sit idle. I hope ye are stronger than ye look, lass?" There was no mistaking the challenge in the older woman's voice.

Davina met Sheena's eye, her mouth curving. "I am," she assured her firmly.

She then fixed her attention on the chieftain once more. "I thank ye, Mackay. I swear I will make myself useful here ... I will not be a burden." And she meant it too. She'd shut herself away at Kilchurn, had let melancholia drown her, but she wouldn't do so here. From now on, she'd be industrious, would contribute to the running of this broch. Davina wasn't a talented weaver, yet she could sew well, and she was adept at managing servants.

The laird favored her with a cautious smile. "I have no fear of ye being a burden," he assured her. "I just worry yer father may have something to say about all of this."

Warmth suffused Davina's chest at the sight of the welcoming chamber that would be hers now.

Swallowing to dislodge the sudden lump in her throat, she smiled.

"Is the room to yer liking, Davina?"

She glanced over her shoulder to find Bonnie standing behind her, her smooth brow furrowed. "The chamber is small ... but I think ye shall find it comfortable."

"I definitely shall," Davina assured her before turning back to the room. It was indeed small, yet not cramped. The chamber was lodged in the tower, above Kerr and Lennox's chambers. It had a hearth to keep her warm in the winter and even a narrow window that looked out across the sound. A servant had rolled the sacking up, letting in a fresh breeze.

A canopied bed dominated the space, while a wash bowl sat on a nightstand in one corner. And under the window, there was a desk and chair.

"I'm happy to let my maid, Elsie, tend to ye in the evenings and mornings," Bonnie said then. "She doesn't usually spend long with me."

Davina turned to the laird's wife. "That's kind of ye, Bonnie," she said softly. "But not necessary. I've gotten used to looking after myself, of late." She paused then, favoring Bonnie with another smile. "I'm no longer 'Lady' Davina ... and in truth, I prefer it that way."

Bonnie's face tensed, and she wrung her hands together. "Are ye certain?"

"Aye." Ironically, their roles were now reversed. Once Bonnie had been a chambermaid and Davina a lady. But now, Bonnie was the lady and Davina was a woman without rank. It didn't bother Davina though—if anything, the change made her feel free.

Nonetheless, Bonnie didn't look happy about the situation. "I want ye to feel at home here ... and welcome."

"And I do."

Bonnie's mouth quirked. "I hope Sheena didn't intimidate ye ... my mother-by-marriage can have a tongue like a blade."

Davina laughed. "Aye, so I've noted. However, she appears to mind *ye*?" Earlier, as they'd waited for the men in the solar, she'd noted that the older woman deferred to Bonnie.

"Aye, well, it was hard won," Bonnie replied, her smile turning rueful. "Sheena didn't believe me worthy of her son when I first arrived." She sighed, her expression sobering. "Iver did warn me, yet her viciousness knocked me just the same."

"Well, I'm glad ye have settled things," Davina replied. "Life for ye here would be wearying indeed if yer mother-by-marriage were against ye." She paused then, surveying Bonnie with interest. "Ye seem far surer of yerself than last time we met. I hoped yer marriage to Iver would be the making of ye ... and it appears it has."

The brilliance of Bonnie's smile lit up the chamber. "Aye," she murmured. "I took yer advice to heart too ...

do ye remember how ye told me that if I was to fit in here, I had to stop believing I was inferior?"

"I remember."

"Well, it was sage counsel and has helped me settle in. Every time I catch myself feeling as if I'm an interloper, I remember yer words."

Davina smiled. "I'm glad to have been of help ... although I must have been gloomy company that day."

Now it was Bonnie's turn to observe her. There was a probing look in her eyes that made Davina a little uncomfortable. "Ye *were* unhappy," Bonnie said softly. "A shadow lay over ye then ... but no longer."

Davina nodded, shifting her gaze away from Bonnie's. "Leaving Kilchurn was a wise decision," she admitted. "There were too many memories there ... too many regrets."

Moving to the bed, her attention rested upon the two saddlebags a servant had brought upstairs for her, and she reached out, her fingertips tracing the worn leather.

All her possessions in just two bags.

It didn't depress her though. Instead, she felt lighter in the knowledge that she could begin again here. She hadn't lied before; she was relieved to leave her title behind her.

"Ye and Lennox traveled quite a distance together," Bonnie said then, drawing her attention once more.

"Aye ... we spent a week on the road together since leaving Kilchurn."

"How did ye find him?"

Davina turned once more, inclining her head. "What do ye mean?"

"Sheena wasn't the only one who disapproved of Iver's choice of bride," Bonnie replied, swallowing. "Lennox was also vexed by it." She paused as if choosing her words carefully. "In truth, I wasn't sure what to make of him."

Davina frowned. "He wasn't rude to ye, was he?"

Bonnie shook her head. "He barely spoke to me ... although on the day we left Kilchurn, he did offer an apology." Her mouth kicked up into a smile. "Rough though it was."

Davina sighed. "He's a complex man," she admitted. "During our journey south, he admitted he sees himself as the black sheep of the family ... he never felt understood. I think that's why he took the position at Kilchurn."

"A position he cast aside to help ye," Bonnie said softly.

There was a glint in Lady Mackay's eye now, one that made Davina's stomach somersault. Her pulse then started to race.

She'd forgotten how astute Bonnie was.

She and Lennox had barely spoken since their arrival, but Bonnie would have noted how easily they met each other's eye during the meeting in the solar. The men wouldn't likely pick up on such a detail—but Bonnie had.

Stop panicking, Davina chided herself. *She doesn't know anything.*

"There's a chivalrous side to him that he fights," Davina replied with a snort, deliberately making light of the comment. "Lennox Mackay pretends he cares about nothing but himself ... but that's a ruse. He missed his family and this broch." She broke off there, her gaze going to the rippling expanse of water beyond and the shadow of the Isle of Arran on the horizon. "And I can see why he did."

24: LIKE OLD TIMES

"DAVINA SEEMS DIFFERENT to how I remember."

Lennox glanced up, from where he sat, his fingers laced around a cup of apple wine. It was getting late, and the four brothers had retired to Iver's solar for a drink before bed.

The sacking had been lowered on the windows, the room illuminated by the glow of the fire and lanterns that flickered on the walls.

"Aye," Lennox replied, lifting his cup, and taking a sip. "She's been through a lot of late." The strong wine warmed his tongue and throat as he swallowed before settling in his belly.

He needed to fortify himself if they were going to talk about Davina.

He'd managed to avoid doing so since his arrival—but now that he was alone with his brothers, he shouldn't have been surprised Iver had brought the subject up. In truth, he'd rather have talked about other things. Relations had been strained between him and Davina ever since Inverneil. He hid it well, but her flat rejection of his proposal had been a slap to the face. He knew she didn't wish to marry, but he'd thought she'd consider letting him take care of her, all the same.

On the contrary, she'd made her position clear.

He'd been nursing his bruised pride ever since. He wasn't used to women like Davina. In his experience, lasses would use any excuse to trap a man into marriage—over the years, he'd learned how to disentangle himself without too much unpleasantness.

But Davina wasn't interested in trapping him—or anyone.

"I recall her as being as pale as a wraith and so fragile a puff of wind would break her," Iver went on, his gaze meeting Lennox's. "But the woman who arrived today had a bloom to her cheeks and a strength to her."

Lennox nodded. "Despite everything, the journey did her good," he replied. "She spent too long locked away, letting regret gnaw at her. If she'd remained at Kilchurn, she'd likely have sickened."

His brothers all nodded at this. However, Kerr's expression was veiled, and Brodie's brow was furrowed.

"Ye did the right thing then," Brodie said after a pause, his voice gruff, "Bringing her here."

Lennox fought a grimace. "I hope so."

"It will be good for Bonnie to have female company of her own age," Kerr added.

"Bonnie is delighted to have Davina's company," Iver said, swirling the wine in his cup gently as he eyed Lennox. "That isn't my concern ... her father is."

Lennox swallowed another gulp of wine. "Davina seems convinced he won't bother with her again ... and I'm inclined to agree with her."

Iver scratched his jaw with his free hand. "Maybe, but ye abandoned yer post, Len. He's not likely to be happy about that. I'd wager he'll demand answers. He'll want to know why ye aren't returning to Kilchurn after making sure Davina is safe, at the very least."

Lennox's gut hardened. Even more than discussing Davina, he dreaded speaking about why he'd come home. "I intend to write to Campbell personally ... and shall explain my reasons," he replied.

Iver's gaze never wavered. "And will ye tell *me*, brother?"

Lennox leaned back in his chair, crossing one leather-clad ankle over his knee. "I thought a fresh start was what I needed ... and perhaps it was." He let his gaze travel to each of his brothers' faces. "But as the weeks slid by, I realized that I was an outsider at Kilchurn ... far more than I'd ever been here."

"Ye were never an *outsider* here, Len," Iver replied, his voice tightening. "This is yer home."

Lennox sighed, favoring Iver with a half-smile. He appreciated the sentiment—and Iver was right. He did belong at Dun Ugadale. Maybe he always had, yet he'd been too restless and pigheaded to see it.

"Did yer men not accept ye?" Kerr asked then.

"They did ... grudgingly," Lennox replied. Nonetheless, he'd been warmed by how Hamish and the others had bid him farewell. Aye, their relationship had been difficult, yet, ironically, the journey had built a bond between them. Had he returned to Kilchurn, things would have been easier.

He drained the last of his wine then and set the cup down on the table next to him. "Kilchurn is a mighty fortress ... and I was honored to serve Campbell, but every time I walked the high curtain wall and looked down over Loch Awe, all I could think about was that the wall wasn't covered in moss and in dire need of repair."

His brothers snorted then, and Lennox's mouth quirked. "Or that I wasn't looking across the glittering waters of Kilbrannan Sound." He paused then, his throat tightening. "And I missed ye all," he admitted roughly.

And he had. As he sat there in the chieftain's solar with his three brothers, a sense of completeness filtered over Lennox. Iver, Kerr, and Brodie knew him better than anyone else. They knew all his faults, yet they accepted him without question.

Iver was now reclining in his high-backed chair, watching him. His elder brother was usually easier to read than Kerr or Brodie, but not so this evening. He wondered then if the rift between them would ever be healed. The Mackays were proud, and despite that he'd welcomed his brother back, Iver *had* been offended when Lennox took up the role at Kilchurn.

"We missed ye too," Brodie said gruffly when the silence drew out.

"The broch *was* dull without ye," Kerr admitted.

"Aye," Iver agreed, his mouth lifting at the corners. "Although I regret to inform ye that the position of bailiff has been filled."

Lennox snorted. He didn't care about that. He'd hated the job. "Whom did ye choose?"

"Kyle MacAlister."

"Kyle is a good man," Lennox replied. He and Kyle were friends, born just a month apart. MacAlister farmed the lands just north of Ceann Locha with his brother. Lennox looked forward to seeing him again.

"Aye, and he's available whenever I need him. The arrangement suits us both."

Lennox snorted. "Well, lucky for ye that Kyle has the hide of a boar ... he'll need it."

Iver merely flashed him a wry smile in reply.

"There's space for ye in the guard, Len," Kerr said then. His brother was watching him steadily, his expression solemn. "If ye won't bristle at taking orders from me?"

Holding Kerr's gaze, Lennox searched for the old resentment, a sensation that had gnawed at his belly like a rat—but this evening, it was absent.

It had been for months now.

It struck Lennox then that he'd wasted far too many years letting old grudges fester. And maybe Iver was right: he'd mellowed a little of late, but as a younger man he'd been impetuous, quick to anger, and always the first to start a fight.

None of those traits would have made him the captain Iver wanted.

"I'll take orders from ye, Kerr," Lennox replied, his mouth tugging into a smile. "If ye agree to let me thrash ye occasionally in the training yard."

Kerr's mouth lifted at the corners. "It'll be like old times then."

Seated in the hall, at the chieftain's table, Lennox helped himself to a slice of roasted venison before heaping mashed, buttered turnip onto his trencher.

Cory's cooking was something else he'd missed while living at Kilchurn.

The cooks there were able enough, but the meals seemed bland compared to those at Dun Ugadale.

He ate slowly, savoring each bite, while listening to the rise and fall of conversation around him. As usual, the hall was busy at this hour. Long trestle tables filled the rectangular space, where warriors sat elbow-to-elbow, laughing and talking as they ate their supper and downed large tankards of ale. Meanwhile, the laird's two wolfhounds positioned themselves at the ends of tables, waiting for food to be 'accidentally' dropped onto the rushes.

It was a mild evening, and so the hearth was cold. Most of the year, a fug of peat smoke hung underneath the blackened beams that crisscrossed the ceiling, but the air was clear tonight, making the hall much more pleasant.

Lennox's gaze slid down the table, past his mother and younger brothers, to where Iver sat upon the carved oaken chair—one that had been made for their great-grandfather. He was deep in conversation with Bonnie.

Lennox watched the couple for a few moments.

There was no denying the connection between them. It was evident in the way their gazes held, the way they let their arms brush and their hands touch as they talked.

Iver looked at his wife as if she were his world, his everything.

Months earlier, his brother's infatuation for the chambermaid he'd bedded at Stirling had vexed Lennox. He'd told himself that Bonnie Fraser had made a great fool of him and had even told Iver he was the laughingstock of the Highlands.

Lennox regretted those callous words now.

Their relationship was no infatuation—anyone could see how devoted they were.

An odd sensation tugged under his breastbone then. For the first time ever, he felt envious of another man's happiness.

Lennox shifted his attention away from Iver and Bonnie to find Davina watching him. Like Lennox, she'd heaped up a generous pile of food upon her trencher. Yet she wasn't eating at present. Their gazes met, and she offered him a smile.

It was a gentle expression—a smile he'd once thought he'd never receive from Campbell's haughty daughter. And in that smile, he saw gratitude.

Lennox swallowed before forcing a smile back.

Curse it, he didn't want her gratitude. He wanted Davina Campbell, in his bed, by his side. He wanted to sit next to her at mealtimes, the way Iver did with Bonnie, to listen to the musical lilt of her voice while being able to reach out and touch her whenever he wished.

The realization jolted through him, and he cut his gaze away, heart pounding.

What the devil?

His fingers tightened around his eating knife.

His return to Dun Ugadale had roused emotions and brought many things to the surface. Things he'd once believed he was immune to.

Reaching for his tankard, Lennox took a large gulp, hoping that it would distract him. It didn't. His stomach clenched, his supper churning, while an ache of longing settled under his breastbone.

Lennox kept his gaze upon his half-finished trencher of food, resisting the urge to look Davina's way again, to let her see the need in his eyes. He had to keep a leash on himself now. He couldn't let his family see him staring at her like some besotted lad.

Davina had made her position clear. She didn't wish for a husband, and now she was safely within the walls of this broch, she didn't need his protection either.

Lennox didn't like feeling spurned, yet he was just going to have to swallow his pride and focus on rebuilding his life here.

He'd always been practical when it came to women, and he would be pragmatic about this too. There wasn't any point in pining for a lass who didn't want him.

25: NO ONE FRIGHTENS YE

DAVINA ARRANGED THE bouquets of meadow flowers carefully before the altar. She then stepped back, her gaze traveling over the buttercups, daisies, and primroses. The decorations were simple, yet they added a touch of much-needed color to the grey-stone kirk.

"Thank ye, Lady Davina." Father Ross stepped up next to her, his kindly face creasing into a wide smile. "The kirk will look welcoming indeed for this morning's service."

"The hills around Dun Ugadale are awash in wildflowers at present," she replied, smiling back. "I couldn't resist gathering some."

Voices reached them then, and Davina glanced over her shoulder to see locals walking up the narrow mossy path, between a scattering of gravestones.

It was Sunday morning—and the inhabitants of the broch and the village beyond were making their way to the kirk.

Leaving the priest to ready himself at the pulpit, Davina moved back and took her place at one of the long wooden benches that lined the kirk. The musky scent of incense mixed with the fatty odor of tallow from the banks of candles flanking the altar filled her nostrils.

Something tugged at Davina then. She'd have been surrounded by these smells daily if she'd been given entry to Iona Abbey. Had Abbess Anna admitted her, she'd be a postulant right now, readying herself to become a novice.

But instead, here she was, living halfway down the Kintyre Peninsula amongst the Mackays, the MacAlisters, and the MacDonalds. Father Ross had told her just a few days earlier that he was a Mackay, a cousin to the chieftain. Indeed, she'd noted he had the same high cheekbones as the chieftain and his brothers. And although the priest's hair was white these days, she wagered it had been blond in his youth.

Shifting on the hard bench, Davina watched men, women, and children filter into the kirk. Their voices were low, respectful, and most of them had made an effort to wash and put on their best clothes.

Davina's mouth curved. Two weeks had passed since her arrival here, and already she was starting to feel at home. She made sure she got out for a walk every day; the fresh air invigorated her, and she never wanted to go back to locking herself away from the world as she had at Kilchurn.

"There ye are." Bonnie slid into the pew next to her. "I was looking for ye."

"I went out early so I could gather fresh flowers for the altar," Davina replied. Her gaze shifted then to where the rest of the family entered the kirk. Villagers respectfully stepped aside so that the laird, his brothers, and his mother could move to the front.

Among them, she spied Lennox. She tried to catch his eye, to smile, yet he wasn't looking in her direction.

Davina's throat tightened. Ever since their arrival, he'd been aloof. Granted, he'd been occupied of late. He'd joined the Dun Ugadale Guard, and he and his brother had been busy training recruits—but whenever their paths crossed, Lennox was painfully polite and made an excuse to leave her as soon as possible.

The day before, she'd even tried teasing him, yet he hadn't risen to the bait as he usually would have.

When she watched him in the barmkin training with the other guards, he was as arrogant as she recalled, with the same swagger and grin that had once infuriated her. But with Davina, he was distant.

I have offended him, she thought, turning her attention back to where the last of the villagers were taking their seats. He'd insisted that wasn't the case, yet his behavior spoke otherwise. A heaviness settled within her then, shadowing her good mood. They both knew that their physical relationship couldn't continue here, yet she'd hoped they could be friends, at least.

But Lennox clearly wasn't interested.

Stop fashing about him, lass, she chastised herself, irritated that her thoughts kept returning to Lennox these days. *Ye have a life of yer own to build here.*

And she did. In the past fortnight, she'd been focused on learning the rhythm and routine of the broch and on finding ways to be helpful. Sheena always seemed to have tasks for her, and Father Ross had welcomed her assistance in keeping the kirk tidy and appealing. She'd also gone out with Bonnie to give alms to the poor and met many of the locals.

Indeed, she caught sight of some familiar faces among the locals this morning. Graham MacAlister and his brood squeezed into one of the pews. The farmer wore a sour expression as he nursed the bound stump of his right wrist—the hand he'd lost for thieving livestock. His three hulking sons had the same look as their father, aggressive and resentful. Unlike most of the congregation, they wore dirty and sweat-stained braies and léines, and their boots were encrusted with mud from the fields. However, his daughter, Rose, stood out amongst them. She wore a fresh blue kirtle, and although the cloth was a little threadbare, the garment was clean. Her face was composed as she took the last place at the pew. Davina spied daisies in her hair.

And as she shifted back to face the altar, Davina noted that Kerr was watching Rose MacAlister.

His solemn face gave nothing away, yet the intensity of his gaze betrayed him. He observed the lass keenly, as if willing her to look his way.

She didn't.

Oh dear, Davina thought. *That's a yearning that can go nowhere.* After witnessing the altercation before the gates of Dun Ugadale upon her arrival, and especially after he'd taken her father's hand off, Rose would likely despise the Captain of the Dun Ugadale Guard. Nonetheless, it appeared that he didn't view her the same way.

The service began then. Father Ross's low voice echoed through the now-silent kirk as he gave his sermon. Its focus this morning was on establishing harmony with one's neighbors. Davina knew his choice was no accident; earlier the priest had confided in her that the continuing discord between the MacAlisters and the MacDonalds worried him.

Indeed, Davina had noted how those two clans kept apart, even now inside the kirk. It was a miracle that they attended Sunday service and suffered to be under the same roof.

"Ye shalt love God with all yer heart, and all yer soul, and with all yer mind—that is the first great commandment," the priest intoned. "And the second is that ye shalt love yer neighbor as yerself."

Davina glanced over at the MacAlisters once more to see Graham's heavy shoulders had hunched. She wagered, even as god-fearing as he was, MacAlister wasn't interested in hearing such wisdom.

The service ended with the taking of the sacrament, where each member of the congregation took a mouthful of bannock and a sip of wine before receiving a blessing from Father Ross.

Once again, Davina wondered what her life would have been like, had she been welcomed into Iona Abbey. Relief washed over her then. Of course, she was never meant to be a nun. Abbess Anna had done her a favor by refusing her entry. Instead, her new life at Dun Ugadale suited her much better.

They then filed outside into the late morning sunshine.

Davina smiled as she walked down the path toward the road that led back to the broch. It had been an odd summer, spells of balmy weather interspersed with wild storms. One such storm had passed a few days earlier, flattening crops and turning the ground soggy—but the sun had returned, and Davina welcomed its warmth upon her face.

Outside the gate to the kirkyard, she waited for the others to catch her up.

Yet, instead of walking with Iver and Bonnie, she fell in next to Lennox.

"That was a fine service, was it not?" she said, favoring him with a shy smile. She was hesitant to seek out his company these days, yet a stubborn part of her didn't wish to let him retreat. Whatever had happened between them, they could still rub along, couldn't they?

"Aye," Lennox replied with a soft snort, "although Graham MacAlister looked like he was about to choke on his tongue when Father Ross started going on about loving one's neighbor."

Davina's mouth pursed. "So, ye noticed that too?"

"Hard not to … the man's glower could curdle milk."

"I suppose it's hard not be resentful when ye've lost yer right hand."

Lennox's gaze glinted. "Well, he should have considered that before continuing to thieve sheep."

Davina arched an eyebrow. His response didn't surprise her. If MacAlister erred again, they'd stretch his neck. Nonetheless, she doubted the farmer held the same view as Lennox.

They were walking through the village now, between squat stone bothies, where washing snapped in the breeze on clotheslines and fowl pecked in the dirt. Goats bleated from enclosures, and bees buzzed around the profusions of flowering herbs surrounding the dwellings.

Davina smiled as she surveyed the village. Despite the tension between some of its inhabitants, it had an air of prosperity.

"Any word from yer father?"

She glanced back at Lennox, to find him surveying her.

Davina's expression sobered, and she shook her head. "Did he ever reply to the letter ye sent him?"

"No." His mouth twisted. "In truth, I thought we'd see him before now."

Her belly tightened. "Well, I did tell ye otherwise."

Lennox's gaze narrowed. "Aye, but I believe, deep down, ye expected him to ride here."

Davina swallowed. She had. Despite everything, she missed her father. She sometimes worried about him and wondered how he was faring. When her mother was alive, she made sure he didn't eat too much salted pork and drink too much mead. Over a year earlier, Davina had warned him that he'd end up with gout, yet he didn't seem to care. "I'm relieved he hasn't," she replied after a lengthy pause—and she was. "No good would come of it."

Silence fell between them then before Lennox asked, "Ye are happy here then, Davina?"

She nodded, glad that he'd changed the subject. "Aye ... Dun Ugadale has welcomed me ... and Bonnie and yer mother have allowed me to make myself useful."

"I heard Cory yesterday," Lennox said, inclining his head, "boasting that the spence has never been so well organized. He says ye spend hours in there, taking stock and sorting."

Warmth rose to Davina's cheeks. She hadn't realized Lennox had been asking questions about her. "Ye know I wish to find real purpose here," she reminded him softly. "Bonnie is often too busy to deal with the spence ... and yer mother terrifies the servants."

Lennox laughed, the rich sound carrying through the air. Up ahead, Iver and Bonnie glanced over their shoulders, their gazes alighting on them. Lennox waited until they'd turned back before he cast a quick look over his shoulder, as if to make sure Sheena Mackay wasn't shadowing him.

"She terrifies everyone," he replied, grinning. "But not ye, I'd wager."

Davina snorted. "I wouldn't say that."

She and Sheena had developed an 'understanding' over the past two weeks. Nonetheless, the woman was as prickly as a hedgehog and could be cutting at times.

"No one frightens ye, Davina," he said softly, a teasing edge to his voice now. "Not even Lucifer himself would."

Davina's smile returned. She couldn't believe she'd missed being teased by Lennox Mackay, but she had. *Lord, I must be going soft in the head.*

Meeting his eye, she inclined her head. "Ye make me sound like a shrew," she replied.

"No." His gaze met hers. "Ye are a warrior. I don't think I've ever met anyone with such an independent spirit. Ye don't need anyone else to be happy, do ye? Just as long as ye have a purpose, ye are content."

She raised her eyebrows. "Now ye are making me sound selfish."

"No, ye are self-possessed ... an attractive trait indeed."

Davina's pulse quickened, heat flushing over her. There was an intimacy to his gaze, one she hadn't seen since that fateful night at Inverneil. It brought back torrid memories—of his hands on her, his mouth tracing across her skin, his shaft buried deep inside her.

Swallowing, she tried to ignore her body's swift response.

Curse it, she'd thought all of that was behind her. She'd spent the past fortnight looking ahead, not behind. She loved living here and didn't want to put it in jeopardy. Lennox shouldn't have looked at her like that, and *she* shouldn't hold his gaze so boldly.

Others would see.

Cutting her gaze away, Davina focused on the high walls that encircled the broch. "Are ye happy to be home, Lennox?" she asked then, desperate to turn the conversation away from herself.

"Aye."

When he didn't elaborate, she chanced another look in his direction. He was watching her, his expression now inscrutable.

"Ye don't find yerself restless, wishing for a different, more exciting life then?" she teased.

"No," he said, breaking eye contact with her, and focusing his attention on the road instead. However, there was an odd flatness to his voice when he continued, "I'm satisfied with what I have."

26: STRUCK BY LIGHTNING

"THAT'S IT, I yield!"

Breathing hard, Kerr threw down his practice sword and raised his hands in surrender. Around them, the warriors looking on cheered.

Lennox scowled. He wasn't ready to stop yet. He still had energy to burn. The muscles in his shoulders and arms were on fire, and he was starting to stagger, yet he wasn't tired enough.

Kerr flashed him a rueful look. His brother's face gleamed with sweat; he'd pulled his shaggy hair back with a leather thong, yet strands had come free, sticking to his cheeks. They'd fought a long while, the dull thud of their bound blades carrying through the barmkin. The fight had gone on so long that, eventually, Brodie had ceased work in his forge and emerged to watch, along with the stable hands.

Their youngest brother lounged against a cart of hay, brawny arms folded across his chest. He wore a thick leather blacksmith's apron, coated with soot and ash.

Catching Lennox's eye, Brodie cocked an eyebrow. "Ye are scrappy today, Len," he observed drily. "Is something amiss?"

"Nothing's wrong," Lennox grunted, wiping sweat from his brow with his forearm. "I was in the mood for a good fight, that's all."

"A good fight?" Kerr snorted. His brother was bent double now, hands braced on his knees as he struggled to catch his breath. "Ye went at me like a berserker."

"Aye," Brodie drawled. "Ye looked as if ye were trying to work off some frustration ... what's the matter, tight balls?"

This comment brought roars of laughter from the warriors and stable hands still gathered around them.

Lennox's jaw clenched. "All right," he muttered. "The spectacle's over."

"Ye heard him," Kerr said, straightening up, his own mouth twitching as he fought mirth. "Get back to yer posts, lads."

The crowd dispersed, leaving Lennox and Kerr still standing in the midst of the barmkin. Brodie hadn't moved either from his indolent position against the hay cart.

Lennox scowled at him. "Don't ye have work to do?"

Brodie nodded, although he still didn't move.

Lennox's lip curled. He wasn't in the mood to be heckled by his brother. Brodie had always been the most observant of the four of them, the quietest who said little but saw much. He'd been crude about it, as men were wont to be—but he wasn't wrong.

Frustration boiled within Lennox this afternoon.

If only Davina hadn't waited for him outside the kirk. He'd done well at avoiding her over the past two weeks. After his realization on the eve of their arrival, about how deep his feelings actually ran when it came to Davina Campbell, he'd buried himself in his new role and succeeded in shoving his disappointment to the back of his mind. He'd even congratulated himself on his self-discipline. No woman would bring him to his knees.

But as they'd walked together away from the kirk, he'd found himself wanting to talk to Davina as he once had. It had been a while since he'd sparred with her, and he'd longed to see those luminous grey-blue eyes spark and her chin lift as she answered him.

Aye, he'd missed her—and the knowledge vexed him. He thought he'd managed to purge Davina from his thoughts, but the truth was, he still wanted her.

Turning away from Brodie, he grabbed a drying cloth and swiped it along his bare arms. Like Kerr, he was dripping with sweat after that swordfight.

The clatter of hooves entering the barmkin made him turn then, his gaze alighting upon the knot of horses approaching. At their head rode a cloaked man with long brown hair seated astride a heavy, feather-footed cob. The new arrival's gaze settled upon the brothers, and his bearded face split into a grin.

"Lennox, ye are back!"

Forgetting his sour mood, Lennox's own mouth stretched into a wide smile. "I was wondering when we'd be graced with yer presence, Kyle."

The bailiff swung down from his horse. He then strode over to Lennox, and the two of them clasped arms in greeting. Kyle MacAlister was a tall and rangy man with a quick gaze and a ready smile. He'd grown up hunting, fishing, and fighting with the Mackay brothers, yet he and Lennox had always been the closest.

Kyle glanced over at Kerr then. "It's been too long since my last visit," he admitted, his smile turning apologetic. "We've been getting the harvest in ... and we had some ewes lamb late this year."

Kerr shrugged. "The laird won't care about that ... just as long as the rents are collected. The king gets twitchy if the clan-chiefs pay their dues late."

"Aye, James needs coin to fund his campaign against the Douglases," Lennox replied, frowning.

Kerr muttered something under his breath about the king using them to pay for his wars, while Brodie scowled.

Kyle pulled a face, making it clear that he agreed with their sentiments before he nodded to where heavy sacks of coin hung from the back of his saddle. "I've managed to collect a large portion of the rents ... although some are still outstanding." His brow furrowed then as he met

Lennox's eye once more. "Any advice on how to get them to pay up?"

Lennox snorted. "It's difficult if folk have no coin to give. Nonetheless, I've got a few tricks ... shall I share them with ye over an ale or two?"

Kyle grinned, slapping Lennox on the shoulder. "Aye ... it's good to have ye back, lad." He then gestured to the coin sacks. "But that ale will have to wait ... I'd better get these rents to Iver."

Lennox nodded before tossing the sweaty drying cloth he'd been using to Brodie. "He's up in his solar this afternoon, doing the accounts ... come on, I'll take ye to him."

"The bailiff has arrived," Sheena Mackay announced as she entered the ladies' solar.

Both Davina and Bonnie glanced up from their sewing.

"Where is Kyle now?" Bonnie asked.

"He's meeting with Iver and Lennox." Sheena moved across to one of the high-backed chairs before the flickering hearth and picked up the embroidery she'd been working on. "Apparently, he's had trouble collecting rents from a few tenants."

"I'm not surprised," Bonnie replied with a sigh. "The rents have gone up. Iver told me the king has demanded a larger tax this year ... to fund his push against the Douglases."

Davina's mouth thinned at this news. Taxes were already high. Despite that her father was a steadfast supporter of the Stewarts, even he grumbled about them. He'd told her that James's father had nearly bankrupted the country with his high taxes and extravagant lifestyle, although his son had been more moderate in his demands—until now.

"What happens if Niel Mackay can't pay the king in full?" Bonnie asked, her gaze widening.

Sheena's expression turned grim. "The crown will send in its debt collectors ... and they'll take whatever assets they need to repay the debt."

"Aye," Davina muttered. "Some clan-chiefs are forced to hand over land ... and they often take it from the chieftains responsible for the shortfall."

Bonnie's pretty face paled at this, and she hurriedly cast aside her sewing. "I'd better go to them ... they will be needing refreshment."

Davina tensed at Bonnie's discomfort. She hadn't wanted to frighten her, but it was easy to forget that Bonnie hadn't grown up in their world. Raised as a servant within the walls of Stirling Castle, she'd never had to worry about paying rent, or the consequences of overdue taxes that many a clan-chief faced.

"There's no need for ye to go," Davina said, jumping up. As always, she was keen to make herself useful. "Ye stay here and finish that léine ... I'll fetch the men some wine."

Bonnie frowned. "Are ye sure? I'm—"

"Of course. I need to get up and stretch my legs anyway."

Leaving the ladies' solar, Davina made her way downstairs to the kitchen, where she fetched a tray of clean cups and a ewer of plum wine. As always, the kitchen was a hive of industry. Cory sweated copiously as he stirred batter for the blaeberry cakes to be served with the noon meal, while around him, the two lads who assisted him chopped vegetables and filled pastry cases. Sunday was a special day, and judging from the toothsome aromas drifting through the kitchen, this meal would be especially delicious.

Davina brought the tray upstairs, navigating the narrow stone steps to the first floor and crossing the landing to the chieftain's solar. She then knocked on the door.

"Come in," Iver's voice reached her.

Pushing the door open with her back, Davina entered.

There were three men present. Iver, Lennox, and a tall, lanky man of a similar age to the brothers. He had long, wind-blown brown hair, a neatly trimmed beard, and twinkling green eyes, and his gaze snapped to her immediately.

Pretending not to notice, Davina glanced over at the laird. "I've brought ye some wine."

"Thank ye, Davina," Iver greeted her. Seated at his desk by the window, a large leatherbound book before him and two small sacks of coin open, the chieftain of Dun Ugadale appeared to be in the midst of counting his rents and checking them off in his ledger. He'd need to send them to his clan-chief soon. Davina remembered her father busy this time of year with the same task, for the king liked to have his taxes delivered by Yuletide.

Moving to the sideboard, Davina began pouring the wine.

"I don't think we've had the pleasure of being introduced," the bailiff said then.

Davina glanced up to find the man observing her. Next to him, Lennox's expression was shuttered.

"Davina Campbell," Lennox said after a brief pause. "May I introduce ye to Kyle MacAlister ... Iver's new bailiff."

"It's a pleasure, my lady," MacAlister said, his mouth curving into a warm smile. He looked as if he wanted to step forward and take her hand, but the fact she was busy with the wine prevented him.

That came as a relief to Davina. She had no wish to encourage suitors.

When each cup was poured, she handed them out—the first to Iver, and then to Lennox and MacAlister.

But when she passed Lennox his wine, their fingers accidentally brushed.

The pulse of heat that passed through Davina made her swallow a gasp. Her gaze jumped to his. The pupils of Lennox's eyes had widened, revealing that he too had felt it.

Their hands hadn't touched since their arrival at Dun Ugadale, and during the days that followed, Davina had told herself that her attraction for Lennox would fade, given time. But that touch had revealed the truth: the pull between them was still as strong as before. She knew it, and now so did he.

Davina's heart started to pound. Heaven help her, this was ill news. She already filled her days with tasks, but maybe she needed to keep even busier—anything to resist the desire that quickened within her.

Fingers tingling, she stepped away and handed Kyle MacAlister his wine.

She then departed the solar without another word.

Lennox watched Davina go, his heart bucking against his ribs.

God's blood. He felt as if he'd just been struck by lightning. His whole body was tingling in the aftermath of that light brush of the fingers, his gut had clenched, and he'd started to sweat.

Davina had felt it too, he was sure of it, for she'd briefly met his eye, her expression startled. But she'd composed herself swiftly before leaving the solar with her usual self-possession.

Aye, she was still attracted to him—but that mattered not. She knew as well as him that the heady lust they shared could get them both into trouble. She'd made her choice, and one thing he'd learned about Davina Campbell was that she was a woman with an iron will. Once she set her mind on something, she wouldn't be swayed.

It was the right decision ... for us both, he told himself, refusing to give in to the longing that gnawed at his gut.

Aye, he'd earned a reprieve when she'd spurned his offer. He didn't need a wife. Indeed, he should make a trip to Ceann Locha and find himself a lusty tavern wench to tumble. Perhaps that would ease the knots in his gut and right his mood.

"That's a bonnie maid if ever I saw one." Kyle MacAlister's voice intruded then, and Lennox glanced his friend's way to see he was staring at the door, where Davina had disappeared. His lips were curved, his gaze appreciative—and the sight made Lennox want to bury his fist in his friend's mouth.

Kyle was widowed and on the lookout for another wife.

The bailiff shifted his attention to Lennox then, his smile widening. "Does the lovely Davina have suitors?"

"No," Lennox replied curtly, aware that his brother's gaze was on him now. Iver's brow was furrowed, his gaze sharp. Lennox's already hammering pulse quickened further. Cods, the last thing he needed was his brother noticing anything amiss between him and Davina. "And she doesn't seek any either."

Kyle's green eyes widened. "Why is that?"

"Davina has suffered much of late," Lennox replied. He didn't want to push things, yet he needed to make sure his friend left Davina alone. "She has sworn never to take a husband."

27: WHEREVER YE GO, THERE YE ARE

"THIS BREAD IS yer best yet."

Smiling under the glow of Cory's praise, Davina replied, "Ye like it then?"

The cook nodded before taking another bite of the crust he'd cut off the loaf and slathered with butter.

Davina's smile slid into a grin. She'd kept herself busy of late but had also taken time to learn how to bake pastry and bread. It was mid-morning, and she'd emerged from the spence to find Cory helping himself to the bread she'd made earlier and left to cool.

The morning had flown, as it did when one was busy. With the passing of the days, Davina had thrown herself into any chores she could get her hands on with zeal. She sewed in a frenzy, repairing and making clothing until her eyes watered from concentration and her fingers ached.

Iver and Bonnie had returned the day before from spending a few days together on the Isle of Arran. While they were away, Bonnie left Davina in charge of many of her tasks. Davina enjoyed the responsibility, and she used the time productively. She cleaned out the spence and took inventory of the harvest stocks, before rolling up her sleeves and helping Cory and the lads cure pork and sausages to fill the larder for the winter. In truth, she wasn't used to assisting in the kitchen and initially had worried she'd be more of a hindrance than a help, yet to her surprise, she discovered that she had a talent for it—especially bread-making.

Cory had been a bit awkward about her presence, at first, but after a few days, the cook relaxed, talking her ear off as they worked, shoulder-to-shoulder.

And he was smiling at her now, his ruddy cheeks bulging from the mouthful of bread. Swallowing, Cory huffed a sigh. "It's a pity none of this is for the broch," he grumbled.

"I'll leave a couple of loaves for ye and the lads," Davina assured him. Hearing this, Cory's assistants, Boyd and Callan, both glanced up from where they were readying mutton pies to go in the oven and flashed her grins. "But I'm taking the rest for the poor."

Cory nodded before gesturing to the large wicker basket hanging from one of the beams overhead. "Ye'll need that one for all that bread," he said, "and mind ye don't linger in the village or ye shall miss the noon meal."

"Aye," Callan piped up, wiping his sweaty brow with the back of his hand and leaving a smear of flour. "They fall upon our pies like wolves ... ye have to get in quick."

Davina laughed. "I shall head off now then." Grabbing the basket, she began loading it full of crusty, fragrant, still-warm bread before carefully placing a clean square of linen over the loaves. "I shall see ye all soon."

And with that, she tucked the heavy basket against her side, resting it on her hip, and left the hot, smoky kitchen.

Stepping out into the barmkin, Davina glanced up at the grey sky. The misty rain had ceased for the moment; it was the perfect time to take a trip down to the village.

She'd been at Dun Ugadale a month and a half. Summer was waning now. The air grew crisp at night, and the sun's heat lessened. The balmy weather had disappeared too, and days of low cloud and drizzle settled over the Kintyre peninsula.

The rumble of men's voices reached her then, followed by the thud of bound blades colliding. Her gaze traveled across the barmkin to where Lennox was leading recruits through sword training.

Running a critical eye over the sweating faces and clumsy moves of the green lads they'd taken on, Davina wondered how long it would take Lennox to get them fighting ready.

Over the past weeks, there had been plenty of talk about the need to strengthen Dun Ugadale's defenses. News had reached them that parliament had absolved King James of any blame for killing the Earl of Douglas earlier in the year—a decision that meant the king could push forward in his persecution of the 'Black Douglases' without worry of reprisal. Several clans were being pulled into the conflict now, and civil war was looming.

The Mackays of Dun Ugadale had to be ready for whatever would come.

Davina's attention shifted to Lennox then.

Despite the cool day, he was dressed in a sleeveless tunic and light braies. Sweat gleamed off his bare arms as he strode amongst the sparring pairs of recruits, correcting their positioning and barking advice.

He tore a practice sword off one of the bumbling lads then, shouldered him out of the way, and demonstrated a feint and parry.

Davina couldn't take her eyes off him. His lithe body moved with fluid precision. He made wielding a sword look easy. It had been a while since she'd focused on Lennox so intently; she should have looked away yet found she couldn't.

They still had little to do with each other these days— sitting apart at mealtimes and barely speaking when their paths did cross. Davina had thought he might seek her out sometimes, but he didn't.

An ache rose under Davina's breastbone then. God's teeth, she missed him. As much as she enjoyed living here, her newfound role wasn't enough. She longed to sit by his side in the evenings, to tease him, and to watch the glint in his eye as he responded in kind.

Her heart started to pound. The truth was this man mattered to her, deeply. As hard as she tried, she couldn't distance herself from him without suffering.

Lord, no.

Lennox shoved the practice sword back into the lad's hands and muttered a few words. The recruit swallowed before nodding vigorously. Lennox then flashed the lad a grin and slapped him on the shoulder.

And then he looked her way.

Across the yard that separated them, their gazes fused.

Davina's breathing caught.

Lennox's smile froze on his face. He clearly hadn't expected to find her there, watching him so boldly. His eyebrows knitted as their stare drew out, his jaw tensing.

Heat washed over Davina in a boiling tide. *What the devil was she doing?*

Yanking her gaze from him, Davina clutched the heavy basket against her side and marched toward the gates. And as she went, she cursed her weakness, cursed the longing that wouldn't let her be.

Walking back from the village later, after delivering the last of her bread to the poor, Davina pushed back her hood and turned her face up to the misty rain.

Noon was drawing near, but she'd be back in time to help herself to one of those famed mutton pies.

Not that she had much appetite—not after her encounter with Lennox earlier.

Her burning embarrassment had faded, although now she just felt weary. Exhaustion pulled at her limbs.

Davina heaved a sigh. Perhaps she'd been pushing herself too hard of late. It seemed as if she was retreating into old habits. Back at Kilchurn, she'd withdrawn into sorrow, barely paying attention to the passing of the seasons—and she'd told herself she'd never let melancholia rule her again. But was her frenzy of activity now any different?

In her desire to carve a place for herself at Dun Ugadale, to forget that stolen night with Lennox on the way here, as well as the disturbing sensations the man still roused in her, she'd found another way to escape reality.

She was still on the run, still searching for an elusive freedom that seemed just beyond her grasp.

Her grip tightened upon the handle of her empty basket.

She was beginning to think that freedom was just an illusion anyway. Becoming a nun would have liberated her from her father's insistence she took a husband, yet the rigid discipline within the abbey would have stifled her eventually. And this life too had its limitations. She was here at the laird's whim, and Iver Mackay could change his mind at any time and send her away.

Swallowing the sudden lump in her throat, Davina picked up her skirts and circuited a large puddle in the road.

Restlessness thrummed through her, and it struck her that, even if she'd been admitted to Iona Abbey, she'd likely be struggling with the same disquiet, the same desire to be somewhere else.

Wherever ye go, there ye are.

Around her, low cloud hung over Dun Ugadale like a pall of heavy smoke, fog creeping in from the sea. Nonetheless, cottars still worked in the fields, harvesting the last of the summer crop, and readying the ground for the winter. Their bent figures appeared almost wraithlike in the gloom.

Davina sighed. Maybe she should ease up on her work a little.

The drum of approaching hoofbeats roused her from her thoughts and made her glance over her shoulder.

A heavy cob was approaching at a canter, mud spraying up behind its feathered hooves. A cloaked figure sat astride it.

Davina quickly moved off the road. She didn't want to be run down or splattered with mud. Yet the rider must have spied her, for the horse slowed to a trot. And when the individual drew up alongside her, they pushed back their hood.

Kyle MacAlister grinned down at her. "Good afternoon, Davina ... it's poor weather to be out for a stroll in."

Davina favored him with a polite smile before motioning to her basket. "I was delivering bread to the villagers."

His eyes crinkled at the corners. "Kind as well as beautiful."

Davina decided to ignore the compliment. She was aware that the bailiff—who'd been widowed two years earlier and left with three bairns to raise on his own— was interested in her. He'd made a few trips to Dun Ugadale of late, and Bonnie had told her, with a knowing glint in her eye, that MacAlister didn't usually favor them with so many visits.

She'd given him no encouragement—but the man persisted.

The pair of them continued up toward where the walls of Dun Ugadale disappeared into the mist.

"I can give ye a ride for the remainder of the way, if ye like?" MacAlister offered after a pause.

"No need," she said, forcing a bright tone. "I'd prefer to walk."

She quickened her pace, hurrying toward the causeway now. However, the bailiff kept up with her.

"Ye are looking well, Davina," he said after a brief pause. "Life on the Kintyre peninsula clearly agrees with ye."

"Thank ye," she replied with another demure smile. "It does."

"Do ye have no contact with yer kin at Kilchurn then?"

She shook her head. She'd been on edge in the first few weeks after her arrival here, half-expecting an enraged Colin Campbell to turn up and drag her home.

But he hadn't. She really was dead to him, after all.

"Yer father hasn't visited?"

"No." Christ's bones, she wished he'd change the subject. She'd made the mistake of telling him about the family rift during his last visit and was now sorely regretting being so candid.

"Ye could write to him, ye know?" Kyle MacAlister murmured then. The gentleness of his voice made her meet his eye. And from his expression, she realized he'd seen the sadness on her face.

"There's no point," she replied, cutting her gaze away and focusing upon where the wickedly sharp teeth of the portcullis yawned before them. "He'd never reply."

28: WE ARE YER FAMILY

LENNOX WASN'T ENJOYING supper.

For one thing, Kyle MacAlister was present. Usually, he liked seeing his friend, but these days, he suspected there was an underlying reason for Kyle's frequent visits to Dun Ugadale.

He wasn't just here to discuss rent collection with Iver—but to woo Davina.

The bailiff had arrived just in time for the noon meal. And since he had a few things to discuss with Iver, he'd stayed on for supper.

And just like at noon, Kyle had seated himself next to Davina.

Casting a glance across at where Davina ate, her gaze downcast, Lennox wished she'd look his way—as she had in the barmkin earlier. She'd taken him by surprise that morning. His focus had been on ensuring the new guards didn't accidentally cut off their own limbs when wielding an unbound blade. But when he'd shifted his attention across the courtyard and seen Davina standing there watching him, the impact of their gazes meeting had driven the air out of his lungs.

He'd done his best to keep his thoughts elsewhere of late, yet all it had taken was a few moments to unravel all his good work.

He'd been out of sorts for the rest of the day.

"The dumplings in this stew are excellent," Kerr commented then, his voice carrying down the chieftain's table and intruding on Lennox's brooding. "Cory tells me ye made them, Davina?"

Glancing up, Davina smiled. "Aye, under his guidance." She paused then, her cheeks growing pink as all gazes at the table swiveled to her. "I'm glad ye like them."

"An able cook too," Kyle said, favoring Davina with a warm smile. "Ye are quite a woman."

Lennox's hand clenched around his spoon. Aye, she was, although if Kyle kept showering her with compliments, he was going launch himself across the table and blacken his friend's eye.

Seated opposite him, bathed in candlelight, she was lovely indeed. Davina had bloomed in the past moon. The angular edges of her face had filled out, and her cheeks had a healthy glow to them. She'd once been rail-thin, yet her figure too had grown more rounded. This eve, she wore a grey-blue kirtle that matched her eyes, and her ink-black hair flowed over her shoulders.

It wasn't surprising that the bailiff was entranced by her. But Kyle's interest galled Lennox. Davina said she didn't wish for a husband, but what if Kyle managed to change her mind? His friend had always been popular with the lasses when they were growing up—and Kyle had a charm that Lennox lacked.

Davina might decide she liked him well enough to take a husband, after all.

Jealousy cramped Lennox's belly at the thought.

His gaze remained upon her, although unlike earlier in the barmkin, she ignored him. Lennox was seated directly in front of her, but she skillfully avoided his eye. He couldn't blame her, for he'd carefully done the same of late. Yet as the light of the cresset on the wall next to her caressed her skin, he wished they would stop playing this cruel game with each other.

This evening, he wanted her to know he cared.

He was glad that she'd settled in well in his brother's broch, and that everyone—even his prickly mother—had accepted her, but his longing for her was twisting him up inside.

Lennox lowered his spoonful of venison stew. Of late, he'd lost his usually robust appetite. Cory's excellent dishes just tasted like ash in his mouth. He'd taken to drinking heavily in the evenings when he played at dice or knucklebones with the other guards. He trained hard too, pushing himself, but it couldn't erase his longing for Davina.

And watching Kyle flirt with the woman he wanted was torture.

"I have yet to hear from yer father, Davina," Iver spoke up then. His brow was furrowed as he met her gaze. "I didn't tell ye, but I sent another missive over a fortnight ago. In it, I requested an answer, but Colin hasn't responded."

Davina stiffened at this news.

Iver's gaze didn't waver. "I fear yer presence here may have caused a rift between us and the Campbells ... and since we're neighbors, I must do what I can do repair it."

Davina swallowed before reaching for her goblet of wine and taking a sip. "I don't want to be the cause of problems between our clans."

"Ye aren't," Lennox said, replying without thinking.

Everyone's gazes, including Davina's, snapped to him.

Heat rolled over Lennox, and he silently cursed his impetuousness. "I wouldn't have brought ye here if I'd believed that," he added roughly.

Iver's frown deepened. "Be that as it may, Campbell's silence is worrying. He should have visited us by now or responded to my last missive at the very least."

"Perhaps ye should visit *him*, Iver," Sheena suggested, viewing her eldest son with a sharp gaze. "Take charge of the situation before it worsens."

Iver's mouth pursed. "Maybe I will, Ma," he replied, although Lennox caught the irritated edge to his voice. He didn't appreciate his mother's insinuation that he wasn't already managing the situation well.

Davina's eyes widened at this proposal, alarm fluttering across her delicate features. "There's no need for that," she said, lifting her chin as she held Iver's gaze. "I will leave."

Next to Iver, Bonnie gasped before throwing her husband a censorious look. "Ye can't!"

Davina shook her head, even as her eyes shadowed. "Iver speaks true. My father's silence is damning. Who knows … he may be rallying his men to attack."

Farther down the table, both Kerr and Brodie's faces tensed at these words, silence falling in the hall.

Davina's expression grew pained. "Da has disowned me, but if I throw myself at his mercy and insist it was *me* who put ye all in a difficult position, relations might then thaw between ye." Her face had gone the color of milk now. Lennox's gut clenched; he knew she had no wish to return to Kilchurn.

Iver scowled. "That's an extreme solution, lass," he replied with a shake of his head. "I fear things could end badly for ye."

"They would," Lennox ground out. His gaze speared Davina's then. "Ye aren't going back there."

Davina's jaw tensed, and he caught the stubborn glint in her eye. "But I can't stay here … not now."

Lennox leaned forward. "Dun Ugadale is yer home, Davina," he answered, his voice low and fierce, "and *we* are yer family now."

Davina stared back at him, her gaze widening at his vehemence.

A brittle silence fell then. Lennox was aware that his family were all watching him as well. He could feel the weight of their gazes, yet he didn't look away from Davina.

Satan's cods, he'd said too much, yet he couldn't help it. He wouldn't have Davina thinking she wasn't welcome here.

Davina retired to her chamber directly after supper.

Often, she'd go to the ladies' solar, where she'd perch on the window seat, surrounded by soft cushions, and sip a small goblet of wine before retiring. She usually had the solar to herself in the evenings—Sheena retired early, and Bonnie joined her husband in the chieftain's solar.

But this evening, she only wished to shut herself away.

Her mood, which had been subdued after returning from delivering bread to the villagers, was now dark.

I bring trouble wherever I go, she thought as she closed the door to her chamber behind her. *I should never have accepted Lennox's offer of sanctuary.*

She had no idea that Iver had sent another missive to her father, one that explicitly requested a response. Colin Campbell's silence now had a weighty edge to it.

Davina's skin prickled. Her father had a temper and could be dangerous when roused. She hoped he hadn't made the Mackays of Dun Ugadale his enemies.

Davina halted in the midst of the room, dragging in a deep breath. As always, her chamber was cozy. Maggie, the chambermaid, had been up and lit the hearth. A lump of peat smoldered, casting the small room in a warm glow. She'd also turned Davina's bed down and placed a basin of fresh water and clean drying clothes on the nightstand.

The folk here had been so kind, she didn't want to bring trouble to this broch.

We are family now.

Lennox's words whispered to her, and tears stung her eyes.

His midnight-blue gaze had ensnared hers across the table as he'd spoken those words. His vehemence had shocked her—and it also reminded her of what they'd shared. From the moment they'd left Kilchurn, Lennox Mackay had been her defender in all things. Even now, when they barely spoke to each other, he was looking out for her.

Lowering herself onto the edge of her bed, Davina covered her face with her hands. Tears still prickled at her eyelids, yet she blinked them back. She wouldn't weep. She'd shed far too many tears over the past years, and it had done her no good. She didn't want to start feeling sorry for herself again. The memory of the melancholia that had once dogged her steps, that had drained the world of color, crashed into her.

Suddenly, Davina couldn't breathe. It was as if the walls were closing in on her, as if the pungent peat smoke were choking her.

She had to get out, to suck fresh air into her lungs. She had to find a way to push down the despair that was clawing at her throat.

Davina launched herself to her feet and crossed to the door, plucking her woolen cloak off the hook behind it. Then, slinging the mantle across her shoulders, she hurried from her chamber.

29: SAFE IN MY KEEPING

HE HADN'T EXPECTED to find her up on the walls.

After supper, Lennox had joined the other guards in the barracks for a game of dice. However, he hadn't been in the mood for it, or for the strong wine they were drinking, and so he'd left them to play while he ventured outside.

The mist wreathed thickly around Dun Ugadale tonight, blocking out the waxing moon as well as the surrounding hills and water. It pressed in, tendrils snaking across the ramparts like the tentacles of a ghostly squid.

The air was damp, with a chill that made him wrap his cloak about him.

Men were keeping watch up here, although the mist drew so close that he could barely make out their figures standing atop the guard towers, schiltrons in hand.

But there was one silhouette that didn't wield a spear.

A slender, cloaked outline standing on the eastern wall, staring out at the bank of fog.

Davina.

Her stance reminded him of how he'd seen her, on their last night at Kilchurn. She'd stood staring in the same direction, lost in thought. She'd cut an ethereal figure then, and she did now.

Lennox paused a moment, watching her, before he quietly moved in Davina's direction. And then, when he was a few feet distant, he murmured her name.

She didn't startle as he'd feared. Instead, she glanced over her shoulder, as if she'd been expecting him. Her mouth lifted at the edges, although her gaze was somber, sad. "Come to order me off the wall and back to my bed?" she asked.

He gave a soft snort. Aye, she too recalled that eve, the first occasion they'd spoken directly. "I don't think so, lass," he replied softly. "I remember how ye responded last time I tried that."

She sighed, turning away once more. "I'm difficult, aren't I?"

"No." He stepped up to her shoulder, his gaze traveling over the wreathing mist. It really was as thick as porridge, curling around them now.

She glanced his way again. "We haven't spoken much of late."

He shrugged. "I've tried to give ye freedom to find yer feet here."

"While I've actively avoided ye."

He winced. The lass still could be painfully blunt. "Am I that odious, Davina?" he asked after a pause, trying to keep the hurt out of his voice. His pulse quickened then. Maybe he was. Perhaps that was why she'd kept her distance.

"No," she whispered. "Ye are strong, proud ... and loyal to a fault."

Lennox jolted. He hadn't expected such praise.

He met Davina's eye then. She wasn't smiling. Instead, her expression was bereft, her eyes deep pools of sadness. "Nothing in life is simple, is it?"

He shook his head.

"When I accepted yer offer, I didn't think about the possible consequences." Her throat bobbed. "What if Da attacks Dun Ugadale?"

Lennox sighed. "He won't."

A groove formed between her eyebrows. "How can ye be so sure?"

"I got to know yer father during my time at Kilchurn," he replied with a rueful smile. "Aye, he can be bullish, but he's not irrational. He may be vexed with me for bringing ye here, and Iver for taking ye in ... but I don't think he'd lay siege to this broch over it."

Reaching out, he took her hand. Her fingers were slender and cold. Too cold. How long had she been standing out here?

However, his words had eased her a little; he saw it in her eyes. The light was dim upon the wall, her lovely face illuminated by the nearby glow of a brazier.

Silence swelled between them before Davina cleared her throat. "I've missed ye," she admitted huskily.

Warmth flushed through Lennox's chest. "Ye have?"

"Aye. Ye aggravate me, Lennox Mackay, ye challenge me ... but without ye, everything just seems ... flat."

Lennox's breath rushed out of him, and he cupped her cold hand between his own, squeezing firmly. "And I've missed ye, lass," he admitted. "Those days we spent together, riding here, brought me alive." He paused there, noting the way her brow furrowed. She didn't understand what he meant. He was going to have to speak plainer. "When I asked ye to be my wife, I told ye it was because I wanted to protect ye," he continued. His pulse was galloping now, his breathing ragged. "But that wasn't the real reason ... the truth of it is that even then I wanted *ye*." He brought her hand up, placing her palm over his hammering heart. "I'm not good with words like Kyle. I know I lack charm and manners ... but surely, this doesn't lie."

Her fingers contracted against the quilted material of his gambeson.

"Lennox," she whispered.

"I'm sick with love for ye," he admitted, his voice hoarse now. "It's a weakness, Davina ... ye could rip out my heart and trample over it if ye wished ... but its yers, nonetheless."

Her breathing hitched, and those plump lips he longed to kiss parted. "It's not a weakness," she said shakily. "It is an honor." She paused then, as she stepped toward him, closing the gap between their bodies. "And for what it's worth, I'd never trample over yer heart. I'd hold it safe in my keeping, forever."

And then, to his surprise, she leaned into him, raised her chin, and kissed him.

Lennox went still, marveling at the pillowy softness of her lips, while breathing in the scent of lavender from her hair.

A heartbeat passed, and another, and then he reached for her, his hands sliding through the silky tresses of her hair to cup the back of her head.

And with a groan of surrender, he kissed her back.

His mouth plundered hers, hot and hungry, while Davina responded with the same fierceness, the same fire.

Her initial kiss had been chaste, but it had only taken a few moments for desire to ignite between them, as it had weeks earlier.

His tongue swept her lips open, and she was lost.

He tasted delicious, just as she remembered. And the feel of his heart, going wild against her palm, unleashed something primal within her.

Something that made her forget everything except Lennox.

He hauled her against him, and she fell into his embrace. Their bodies melted together, and he became her world. Davina's hands slid up his chest, and she clutched at his shoulders.

The kiss deepened further, and as she pushed her hips against him, the iron strength of his erection strained against her belly.

Davina gasped, her hand shifting down to stroke him through his braies.

"Not here." Lennox grasped hold of her wrist. "It's too exposed ... anyone could see."

Emerging from the haze of desire, Davina blinked. Of course, he was right. Despite the enshrouding mist, guards stood at their posts just yards away. They had no privacy on the wall.

Still holding her wrist, Lennox shifted back and led Davina off the wall.

Wordlessly, they descended the steep moss-covered steps to the barmkin. There was no one about at this hour in the cobbled courtyard; even Brodie's forge was dark. Lennox didn't lead her across the barmkin back to the broch itself as she'd expected. Instead, he took one of the burning torches, hanging from a chain on the damp wall, and led her into a small building tucked under the eastern wall.

The smell of iron, wood, leather, and oil greeted Davina, and the ruddy light of the torch illuminated neat rows of helmets, spears, and swords. He'd led her into the armory. A bench ran along one side of the space, where the men stood while they polished their weapons.

Lennox placed the torch in a brace next to the door and turned to Davina.

For a few instants, they merely stared at each other, drinking each other in, and then they both stepped forward, their bodies colliding.

Their mouths met with renewed hunger, their hands tearing at each other's clothing. Their cloaks fluttered to the ground, and then Lennox was undoing the laces of her kirtle. He growled with frustration as the laces knotted, while Davina yanked up the hem of his gambeson and léine, fumbling with the laces to his braies. With a curse, Lennox ripped the front of her kirtle open and then shoved the garment, and the léine under it, down.

Her breasts popped free, straining toward him, and Lennox stared down at them, his thumbs caressing her hard-pebbled nipples. "Ye have such delicious tits, Davina," he murmured. "I've dreamed of tasting them again." And with that, he lifted her onto the bench. He then stepped close, bowed his head, and took one stiff peak into his mouth, sucking it eagerly.

Davina's gasp filled the armory, her eyes fluttering shut as she gave herself up to sensation.

His hot, eager mouth undid her, as it had back at Inverneil. It shed all her cares from her—all worries for the future, and all regrets for the past. When he touched her, nothing but this instant mattered.

He suckled her harder then, and she arched against him. She began scrabbling at his clothing once more, frustration pulsing through her. "Please, Lennox," she gasped. "I need to touch ye."

Panting, he ripped his mouth from her breasts and shrugged off his gambeson and léine. The torchlight illuminated the hard lines of his body, and Davina's hands traced across the planes of his chest, before sliding down to his belly and the vee of muscle that led down to his groin.

Her blood thundered in her ears as she undid his braies. His shaft sprang free, rock hard, its crown swollen with need. She wrapped her fingers around it, marveling at the satiny skin and the steel underneath.

She slid her hand down its length, thrilling as he groaned low in his throat.

Continuing, she gazed down at where his magnificent rod grew larger still, moisture beading on its head. Images of that wild night at Inverneil returned then, as she'd sat astride his face while she took his shaft deep into her mouth, working him until he spilled.

She wanted to do it again.

Davina wriggled forward, intending to climb off the bench and sink to her knees before him.

Yet he stopped her, stepping back so that she released his throbbing shaft.

"No, lass," he growled. "I haven't finished with ye yet." The sensual promise in his voice made her shiver. Her whole body was alight now, her limbs trembling.

"Lean back," he instructed. Pushing her skirts high around her waist, Lennox spread her wide, exposing her to him.

And then he stared down at her, his chest heaving now. "Look at ye," he growled. "Beautiful."

The intensity of his gaze made her squirm, yet when he slid his hand between her thighs and stroked her with his fingertips, she forgot about being embarrassed. She forgot about anything but the glide of his touch.

His fingers found the exquisitely sensitive nub of flesh there, circling, stroking, and rubbing until her gasps and moans filled the armory.

Davina's head fell back, knocking against the wall. She barely noticed though, for warm, throbbing pleasure gathered in her loins, radiating out from where he stroked her.

And when he slid the slick tip of his rod between her thighs, pleasure twisted low in her belly, gathering and coiling.

"Please," she choked. "Now!"

Back in Inverneil, they'd taken some time to get to this point, but tonight there was an urgency to their coupling. Tonight, the urge to join with him, to have him buried deep inside her, made Davina want to crawl out of her skin.

He didn't argue with her, didn't prolong her agony.

Instead, Lennox grabbed hold of her hips and tilted them up toward him. And then, he thrust into her, sliding to the hilt in one go.

He was big, yet she was ready for him. She wrapped her legs around his hips and drew him even harder against her, welcoming the aching sensation that followed.

Rolling her hips, she whimpered. "Lennox," she breathed. "This feels even better than last time."

"Aye, angel," he ground out, sweat glistening on his face now. "Ye have no idea how often I've taken myself in hand of late … wishing I was buried inside yer tight, hot quim."

Davina gasped. Mother Mary forgive her, how his lusty words inflamed her.

Lennox slowly pulled back then, letting his shaft withdraw almost to the tip. He stilled, his gaze ensnaring hers. "This isn't going to be gentle, lass," he warned her.

Her lower belly melted at these words, an ache throbbing deep in her womb. "Good," she rasped back. "Show me no mercy."

Grunting a curse, he pinned her legs wide and slammed home once more. He then plowed her in deep, powerful thrusts. At first, Lennox stared down at where their bodies met as he took her, but as sweat slicked their bodies and the friction caught fire, he unraveled. He grabbed Davina by the hips, pounding and grinding into her while she writhed under him.

Davina clung to his broad shoulders as he rode her. Each deep stroke brought her higher, closer to oblivion. She was both melting and catching fire at the same time.

Their mouths collided once more, their kisses rough and feverish—and when he took her over the brink, Davina cried out into his mouth. But he wasn't yet done, and he sank deep into her, again and again, drawing out her pleasure. Ecstasy rolled over Davina, rippling out from her loins. She shuddered, so wet now he almost slid out of her.

Lennox drove deep once more, and she wrapped her legs hard around him. He went rigid then, his spine arching, his own raw cry muffled against her lips.

They clung together in the aftermath, the hunger and power of their coupling leaving them both speechless.

It took a while for the slow throb of pleasure in her womb to subside, and meanwhile, a languorous torpor seeped through Davina's limbs.

She basked in it, her lips curving in satisfaction as Lennox's arms went around her. She nestled her face in his sweat-damp shoulder, enjoying the feel of him still buried inside her.

And eventually, when he drew back and sought her gaze with his, his dark-blue eyes gleamed with emotion. "There's no going back after this," he whispered.

"No," she replied, her lips tugging into another smile. "There's no denying I love ye, Lennox."

His breathing hitched—and then, to her surprise, a single tear trickled down his cheek. His chest heaved with emotion.

His reaction moved her, and she reached up, her fingers smoothing the warm droplet. "I know it's been a wee while since ye proposed to me," she said huskily, her ribs constricting. "But if the offer still stands, I'd like to accept."

30: WILD SEAS

SURPRISINGLY, THEIR NEWS didn't shock anyone.

Lennox's brothers all smiled when he told them that he was to take Davina as his wife. Iver's gaze glinted as he slapped him on the back. "I knew it."

"How?" Lennox demanded. He was genuinely taken aback by Iver's response, and by the wide grins now on Kerr and Brodie's faces.

"I'd suspected ye had fallen for the lass," Iver replied, his smile turning wry. "But after yer words last night at supper, I was certain."

Lennox snorted in response.

The brothers stood in Iver's solar. It was early, and servants were bringing in wheels of bannock, freshly churned butter, and heather honey and laying them out on the rectangular oaken table that dominated the space. Shortly, the women would join them.

Stepping close to Lennox, Iver placed a hand on his shoulder. "I give ye and Davina my blessing." He paused then, his gaze shadowing. "However, I have no idea how Colin Campbell will respond to this news."

Lennox's mouth curved, even if his gut tightened at the warning in his brother's voice. "Don't worry, I shall deal with Colin," he assured him.

Iver cocked an eyebrow. He looked as if he was about to say something else, yet Brodie stepped forward and pulled Lennox into a hard hug. "Congratulations, Len," he said, stepping back so that Kerr could embrace Lennox as well. "I'm glad to see ye both came to yer senses ... yer miserable faces were bringing the whole broch down."

Lennox laughed, even as warmth flooded across his chest. He felt a trifle foolish, for he'd believed he'd hidden his longing for Davina. He'd also convinced himself she'd put him behind her.

How had they both been so blind?

"I'm happy to perform the service in the hall, whenever ye are ready," Iver offered then.

"Davina wishes to wed on the steps on the kirk," Lennox replied with an apologetic smile. "She has become friends with Father Ross, it seems."

Iver nodded. "Of course."

The soft patter of footsteps intruded upon their conservation, and Lennox turned to see Bonnie, Davina, and his mother enter the solar. The first two women were smiling, their eyes alive with joy—while Sheena looked quietly pleased.

Bonnie crossed to Lennox and clasped him in a tight hug. "Congratulations to ye both!"

She drew back, her eyes shining. "It gladdens my heart to see ye and Davina so happy. I *knew* there was something up between ye two."

"Aye," he murmured, touched by Bonnie's warm response. His brother had indeed chosen well in Bonnie; she had an open, loving soul. "I didn't realize that we were both so transparent."

His gaze met Davina's over Bonnie's shoulder, and she gave him a soft smile. "Neither did I," she admitted.

Lennox's gaze shifted to his mother then, as Bonnie stepped aside. "Ma?" he said, moving across to her.

Sheena gave a soft snort, even as her lips curled at the edges. "It was about time ye found yerself a wife, Len," she said archly. "I was wondering if ye'd ever meet a woman strong enough to tame ye ... but it seems ye have."

Davina laughed at this, while warmth rose to Lennox's cheeks. "No one's *tamed* me, Ma," he muttered.

Stepping closer to his mother, he enfolded her in a hug. Sheena wasn't one for displays of physical affection, and initially, she went as stiff as a board. But as the hug drew out, she eventually relaxed against him. "Congratulations, my son," she murmured.

"The surcote needs mending," Sheena Mackay muttered, "but I suppose it'll do."

"It's perfect." Gazing at her reflection in the looking glass, Davina smiled. She'd only brought a small selection of clothing with her from Kilchurn—for she'd been expecting to have to relinquish it all upon entering Iona Abbey. There was no time to get a kirtle and surcote made; she and Lennox were getting married at noon today.

But Sheena had come to her rescue. The two women were both tall, and now that Davina had put on a little weight, they were of a similar size.

The surcote wasn't of the latest style, but it was gorgeous: wine-red damask with a fitted waist and long bell sleeves. Under it, she wore a kirtle of rich gold. It had a daring neckline. Around her hips, Davina had fastened a heavy gilded belt, also Sheena's.

Davina glanced away from the looking glass then, observing the two women standing in the chamber adjoining the ladies' solar. This was Bonnie's wardrobe, where she kept her clothes and dressed in the mornings.

Bonnie clasped her hands together and flashed Davina a wide smile. "Ye are right ... it is perfect. The gown fits ye like a glove."

Next to her, Sheena appeared a little less enamored. She was a woman of exacting standards. "Aye, but the hem of the surcote is frayed. It looks shabby."

"Not to worry," Bonnie said brightly, crossing to her sewing basket. "I have some red ribbon we can use to repair it." Grabbing the basket, she pulled up a stool next to Davina and picked up the hem of the surcote. "This shouldn't take long."

Davina smiled down at her before glancing up at the woman who'd soon be her mother-by-marriage. "I do appreciate ye lending me a gown."

Sheena nodded. "Aye, well, a woman should feel bonnie on her wedding day."

A tangle of excitement and nervousness fluttered up within Davina at these words. It felt as if someone had set a basket of butterflies loose inside her.

In just a few hours, she would be Lennox Mackay's wife.

Everything was moving swiftly now, yet nothing had ever felt so right.

Even with Blair? The question arose, and she lowered her gaze, watching as Bonnie's deft fingers attached a silky dark-red ribbon to the surcote's hem.

It wasn't a fair question—nor was it fair to compare the two men.

What she'd shared with Blair Cameron was a first love, one that was heady and forbidden. Their time together had been stolen. Although they'd known each other for years, they hadn't been able to spend hours talking and getting to know each other in the way Davina had with Lennox.

Blair had seemed perfect in every way to Davina, the romantic hero of the tales her mother used to tell her. But no one was faultless. Lennox Mackay had taught her that. The man had many rough edges, yet so did she.

Drawing in a deep, fortifying breath, Davina glanced up, her gaze fusing with Sheena's. "I love yer son, ye know," she murmured.

Sheena smiled at this declaration, warmth filtering over her usually austere face. "I know," she replied.

31: THE WEDDING GIFT

IT WASN'T THE best weather for a wedding—clouds still
enshrouded Dun Ugadale and a misty rain fell in a fine
veil across the land—yet Davina didn't care.

She couldn't stop smiling as she stood upon the stone
step before the kirk, her hands clasped in Lennox's.

Likewise, he smiled down at her, their gazes never
wavering while Father Ross spoke the words that bound
them.

Meanwhile, a small party gathered before the kirk:
Lennox's brothers, Bonnie, Sheena, and a few servants
from the broch, including Cory, the cook. Some of the
villagers had also approached the kirk as the bell tolled.
Rosy-cheeked women, woolen shawls wrapped around
their shoulders, looked on as Lennox spoke his vows,
and Davina followed suit.

And then, Father Ross's gravelly voice carried
through the misty rain. "I now pronounce ye husband
and wife."

The priest unwrapped the ribbon of Mackay plaid
that he'd knotted around their joined hands and stepped
back, a wide grin splitting his face. "Go on, Lennox …
give yer wife a kiss."

Laughter erupted amongst the watching crowd,
although Lennox paid none of them any mind.

Instead, he stepped forward and gathered Davina in
his arms. His smile softened to an intimate, tender
expression that made her pulse stutter. This man kept up

a front most of the time yet was capable of such deep emotion.

And now, he wasn't afraid to show it.

"With pleasure," he murmured. And then his mouth slanted across hers.

The kiss drew out as he bent Davina back.

She was vaguely aware of his brothers' cheers and catcalls, and when Lennox finally released her, heat flamed across her cheeks. He put an arm around her shoulders, whispering in her ear. "Ye look lovely, angel ... dressed in red with golden buttercups in yer hair."

Davina leaned into him. "Ye can thank yer mother and sister-by-marriage for that," she replied. Indeed, with Sheena and Bonnie's help, her wedding gown was something to behold. Bonnie had even ventured out, not letting the light rain hinder her, and picked buttercups from the hills surrounding the broch. She'd then woven the golden-yellow flowers, which matched the kirtle Davina wore under her surcote, through Davina's black hair.

The final effect made her look as if she wore a fairy queen's crown.

Turning, they faced the gathering waiting before the kirk. Iver and Bonnie stood together near the front, their faces alive with joy—and Davina's throat constricted.

"I really am part of yer family now," she whispered to her husband.

"Aye," he replied huskily, his grip on her tightening. "Davina Mackay."

The thunder of approaching hoofbeats intruded then, penetrating the circle of smiles and laughter in front of the kirk.

Davina stiffened against Lennox while she peered through the swirling mist. Likewise, Iver, Kerr, and Brodie drew the dirks they carried at their waist. She knew it was just a precaution, yet the sight made Davina's heart kick against her ribs—and when horses and riders emerged from the fog, her skin prickled.

There was something about the way the lead rider crouched low over his horse's neck, his coal-black hair, laced with grey, streaming behind him, that was familiar.

Her breath hitched before she gasped. "Da!"

Next to her, Lennox whispered a curse.

Colin Campbell was riding at a gallop, yet upon spying the rickety fence that encircled the kirk and the graveyard surrounding it, he pulled his courser up. The poor beast was lathered, its nostrils flaring. Likewise, the band of men that followed the Lord of Glenorchy drew their mounts to a halt. Davina recognized her father's guard—Hamish and the others who'd escorted her to Iona.

They all dismounted, and then Campbell untied something from behind his saddle before striding toward the wedding party.

Davina's gaze remained fixed upon her father.

She'd thought never to see him again, but here he was, sweat-stained, his clothing wet from riding. Her belly clenched then, for his expression was formidable.

"Colin." Iver stepped away from Bonnie and moved forward to greet him. "I've been expecting ye."

"Apologies for not responding to yer missives, Mackay," Campbell growled halting a few yards back from the laird. "However, other matters have held my attention of late." His gaze cut to where Davina still stood, at Lennox's side, upon the step of the kirk. "I finally make it to Dun Ugadale and ride up to the broch … only to discover there's a wedding taking place this morning. What's this, daughter?"

Davina readied herself to answer. But Lennox spoke first. "There is indeed a wedding, Colin … Davina's and mine." His voice was level, yet Davina caught the wary edge to it. Who knew how her father would react?

Queasiness rolled over Davina. There was no other response Lennox could give, but knowing her father's volatile temperament, it was best to brace themselves for the worst.

Campbell's heavy brow furrowed, his broad shoulders bunching. Behind him, his men's faces, even Hamish's, were grim. "Is that so?"

"Aye." Davina found her tongue then. "Ye are just in time to offer us yer well-wishes, Da." She kept her voice light, even as her pulse went wild. Cold sweat beaded on her skin.

Heavens help her, she was cursed. It was as if Fortuna delighted in throwing obstacles in her path. Would her father fly into a rage? Would he draw his dirk and try to kill Lennox, as he had Blair?

He was capable of it.

Breathing hard, her father lifted the sack he'd untied from behind his saddle, holding it aloft. Davina's gaze seized upon it, her stomach roiling when she saw dark stains—blood—soaked through the coarse material. "I bring ye a wedding gift then," he ground out.

He then threw the sack at them.

It landed on the ground before the steps to the kirk. The top wasn't secured and so the object within rolled out onto the muddy ground.

A severed head.

Gasps went up around them, the women placing horrified hands to their mouths, while the men muttered curses.

It was already decaying, and bloodied, yet the face—twisted into a grotesque expression—was still recognizable.

Bile surged, stinging the back of Davina's throat. Dizziness assailed her, and she grasped Lennox's arm. It had gone as hard as iron under her grip, betraying his shock.

"Brogan Douglas." Lennox's gaze never left the grisly trophy. "Ye caught him then?"

"Aye." Her father's tone was triumphant. "I wasn't going to let that sack of shit rob my daughter of her dowry. After the lads returned to Kilchurn, we set out north and picked up his trail once more." His gaze glittered. "And eventually, we found him."

Silence followed these words, while Campbell met Davina's gaze. "He'd already handed the coin over to his treasonous cousin ... but I took my vengeance nonetheless." He paused then, his face twisting as if he was in pain. "I did it for ye, lass."

Davina swallowed. "Thank ye, Da." Her heart was still pounding, and she felt sick to her stomach, but something in her father's voice eased the dread that twisted her insides.

Was she imagining it, or was Colin Campbell trying to apologize?

"I'm glad ye found him," Lennox said, his tone still guarded. "And I hope his death wasn't a clean one."

Campbell flashed him a violent smile, showing his teeth. "No." He moved forward then, ignoring where Iver, Kerr, and Brodie all stood, dirks still drawn, watching him. Instead, Campbell's gaze speared Lennox's. "Ye abandoned yer post, Mackay," he rumbled. "Ye swore an oath to me, or have ye forgotten?"

"No," Lennox replied quietly. "I haven't."

"So, what say ye?"

Lennox stared back at Davina's father, the air between them crackling as if lightning were about to strike. "I made a choice, Colin," he replied. "Davina was in trouble. The abbess at Iona denied her entry, and she was going to remain in Oban and try to scratch a living on her own. I couldn't let her do that. I had to protect her."

Davina watched her father's brows knit together, watched a storm brewing in his blue eyes. "She could have come home."

"No," Davina said softly. "Ye turned yer back on me, Da ... do ye not remember?"

Her father's gaze shifted to her, his heavy features tightening. "Lass," he said hoarsely. "I made a mistake ... I'm sorry."

Davina started. She couldn't believe it; her father *was* apologizing. He knew he'd erred. This was the first time he'd ever humbled himself before her. It was shocking.

Campbell glanced back at Lennox then. "So, ye brought Davina back here and wed her, to *protect* her?" There was no mistaking the challenge in his voice.

"No," Lennox replied, his own tone hardening. "I married her because I love her."

Whatever her father had been expecting to hear, it wasn't this. His eyes widened, and a nerve jumped in his cheek. Moments passed, while the rain fell in a silent veil around them.

None of those looking on uttered a word, and Davina was grateful. They'd reached a crossroads now. Everything depended on what happened next.

Campbell's attention moved back to her then, his gaze questioning. "Didn't ye swear never to wed?" he reminded her, his tone gruff.

"I did," she replied, her mouth curving ruefully. "But just like ye, Da, I discovered I was mistaken about a few things." His grizzled eyebrows raised at her pert response, yet she continued. "Lennox has helped me open the doors to the cage I built for myself." She glanced at her husband then, to find his gaze upon her, his eyes gleaming. "He accepts me, loves me, for who I am, just as I am."

Davina broke off then, focusing on her father once more. Tension gathered in her chest as she waited for his answer.

Campbell's gaze narrowed further as he surveyed her. "Ye *are* different," he rumbled. "Ye remind me of how ye used to be ... before ..." He cleared his throat then before dragging a hand over his face. Suddenly, her father looked older, tired. "I know ye think I'm a heartless beast, lass ... but I *do* care what happens to ye. Sending ye away broke my heart."

Something splintered within Davina at these words.

She let go of Lennox's arm and descended the kirk steps. Four strides brought her around Brogan Douglas's severed head, and then she threw herself into her father's arms.

He stank of sweat, wet wool, and leather. His big body stiffened in surprise before his arms went about her, squeezing tight. "Careful, lass," he said hoarsely, "or ye'll dirty yer pretty gown."

Davina snorted a laugh as she wrapped her arms around his barrel chest. "I don't care about that," she replied. And she didn't. He was her father, and despite everything, she loved him. "I'm glad ye are here, Da." Her voice roughened as she drew back and tilted up her head, her gaze meeting his. "Will ye stay awhile?"

He stared down at her, his heavy features softening. "Aye, lass."

32: TROUBLE LIES ELSEWHERE

THERE WERE A few moments that Lennox wished he could grab hold of so that he could slow time just for a short while.

This evening was one such occasion.

Outside, the weather was grey and gloomy, and the drizzle had increased to a steady downpour. Indoors, the air was damp and pungent with the odor of wet wool, too many bodies pressed close, and peat smoke. His brother's hall was packed. They'd just finished the wedding feast—a delicious meal of roast blood sausage, roast venison, and braised kale and onion, served with an array of breads.

Cory hadn't been given much notice, yet he and his lads had worked miracles. He'd even managed to find time to bake small cakes, soaked in a rich honey syrup— and when he served them to Davina and Lennox, his face beaming with pride, the bride's response made him grin from ear to ear.

Davina had uttered a moan of pleasure as she took a bite, and as she finished the first cake, Lennox hadn't been able to take his eyes off her. Afterward, she daintily licked her fingers—and Lennox continued to stare, transfixed by her darting pink tongue.

His groin started to throb, and suddenly, all he could think about was hauling her upstairs to his chamber, leaving the rest of the hall to celebrate in their absence.

But he didn't.

Instead, he ate his own honey cake and fed his wife another.

Davina's gaze met his now as she licked a crumb off his thumb, and the sensual promise in her eyes made his breathing grow shallow.

"Keep looking at me like that, lass, and I shall forget myself and take ye, here and now, on the table."

She laughed, although her gaze glinted, almost as if she dared him to.

Lennox's already aching groin swelled further. Curse it, he wouldn't be able to walk in this state, let alone dance. He'd just noticed one of the men had retrieved his Highland pipe and was readying himself to play.

Meanwhile, others were folding up the trestle tables and placing them against the walls, making space for the dancing to come.

Around them, bursts of laughter punctuated the rumble of conversation. It was so loud in here that Davina and Lennox had to lean close to hear each other. Not that Lennox minded though; it just gave him an excuse to reach out and touch his wife, to brush his lips over her ear.

Desperate to lower his embarrassing state of arousal, Lennox reached out and picked up his goblet before taking a sip of rich bramble wine. His gaze then slid around the chieftain's table, surveying his family and their guest.

Colin Campbell sat between Iver and their mother. His cheeks flushed with wine, he appeared to be attempting to flirt with Sheena.

Lennox's mouth curved at the sight. His mother was around ten years Campbell's elder, yet she was still a handsome woman. And their age difference didn't seem to be putting him off. Watching them, Lennox was surprised to see his mother didn't look vexed.

She didn't appear overjoyed by the attention, yet judging from the way Campbell was responding to her, she hadn't flayed him with her tongue either.

"I never expected yer father to give us his blessing," Lennox said, leaning into his wife once more.

"Me neither," Davina replied, her attention flicking to the opposite end of the table, where Campbell was eagerly refilling Sheena's goblet with wine. "There's a change in him ... although I cannot say exactly what it is."

"I can," Lennox replied. "He's a man humbled ... who wishes to make amends for his mistakes. That's why he rode after Brogan Douglas ... why he brought ye his head." He grimaced then. "Yer father isn't a man to do things by halves."

"No," she said softly. "But then, neither are ye."

Lennox smiled, shifting his focus back to his wife. "Ye are happy, I think," he noted, "to make peace with him."

Davina nodded. "After everything, he's still my father."

"He is." Lennox took her hands, lacing his fingers through hers. "And it's clear he does actually love ye."

The wail of the Highland pipe sliced through the din then as the piper began to play a lively jig.

"Come on, Lennox!" Iver shouted down the table. Seated with his arm around his wife, the chieftain grinned at his younger brother. "Get yer arse out onto the floor ... the wedding couple has the first dance."

Lennox stifled a groan.

Fortunately, his throbbing erection had subsided a little, thanks to shifting his focus elsewhere. Even so, he preferred to watch others dance rather than take part. The only time he danced was when he'd downed a skinful. Indeed, the last occasion was at Stirling Castle months earlier when he'd been imbibing a surfeit of rich French wine.

Yet all three of his brothers were banging their pewter goblets on the tabletop now. Kerr's face was flushed with drink, and he looked like he was going to pitch forward, face first into the last of the honey cakes at any moment. Next to him, Brodie's usually dour expression had softened a little, his own gaze glazed from all the wine he'd consumed. He flashed Lennox a lopsided, knowing smile.

All his brothers knew he didn't dance.

Laughing, Davina rose smoothly to her feet, pulling him with her. "Come, husband," she said, her voice teasing. "Let's give them what they want."

Their gazes met, and his grip on her hand tightened.

Aye, he wasn't much of a dancer, but just a couple of months ago, he couldn't have imagined this day would arrive—that he'd love anyone as fiercely as he did this woman.

Davina brought out the best in him. Before they'd set out from Kilchurn, he'd been restless and self-absorbed. Lost. But she'd made him take risks, made him question his motives, his desires.

He didn't know what true honor was until he met her, but he did now. He loved how she interacted with him. Davina challenged him in everything—and now, she was daring him to dance with her.

"Very well, angel," he said, favoring her with a roguish wink. "Are ye ready to give them a show?"

Gasping, Davina collapsed on Lennox's sweat-slicked chest.

She'd just ridden him, hard, upon the sheepskin spread out before the glowing hearth in his chamber. Their coupling had been fierce, almost desperate, and their ragged breathing now blended with the crackling of the fire and the pattering of rain on the wall outside.

Lennox whispered an endearment in her ear, his fingertips trailing down her spine as he held her close. Burying her face in the curve of his neck, Davina smiled.

She was a lucky woman, indeed.

As much as she'd enjoyed the wedding feast and the dancing—and as pleased as she was that her father had joined them—she'd been impatient to leave.

Every time Lennox's gaze hooded while they were speaking, every time his knee brushed against hers under the table or his breath feathered against her ear when he leaned close to tell her something, desire arrowed through her core.

The dancing had been a diversion. Lennox wasn't a natural dancer, yet his lean body moved easily, and he was happy to let her teach him. He ignored his brothers' teasing as he fumbled through some steps.

However, each time his arm snaked around her waist, or his fingers trailed across her wrist, Davina's breathing hitched. The touches teased her, bringing the frustration within her to a boil.

It had been a relief when Lennox had finally led her off the dance floor and—instead of taking her back to their seats—scooped her up into his arms, heading toward the stairs.

Whooping and cheers had followed them, yet Davina hadn't been embarrassed. All she'd cared about was that it was a long climb up to the tower, to Lennox's chamber, and she wanted him now.

And she'd had him.

Sighing, Davina caressed the firelit lines of his chest with her fingertips. "This," she said, sliding down and brushing his nipples with her lips. "Was the best day of my life."

"Aye," he said huskily. "As it was mine."

She propped herself up on an elbow and regarded him. "So, what happens now?"

His mouth quirked. "Christ's bones, ye are insatiable, wife. I'm afraid ye shall have to wait a few moments before I can swive ye again."

She gave him a playful slap. "I wasn't talking about that," she huffed. "I meant, what will happen to *us*? Will we continue living in the broch now that we're wed?"

He inclined his head. "What would ye prefer, love? Iver wouldn't mind if we built a cottage in the village ...

but I'm equally content to reside here if ye wish it." His expression was tender, his gaze soft. He really did want this to be her choice.

Davina considered his words. Part of her was eager for them to have their own household. However, she also enjoyed the community and kinship she'd found inside the broch. Bonnie had become a good friend, as had Cory.

"We can stay here for the moment," she said finally, "although if Iver would one day grant ye land, we could have our own broch."

Lennox grinned. "I like a woman with ambition." He reached up, brushing a lock of hair out of her eyes. "I admit yer idea intrigues me ... and I shall speak to Iver about it." He paused, his thumb smoothing across her chin. "And in the meantime, I shall remain with the guard. Kerr and I work well together."

"Ye do," she murmured. Despite her best efforts to avoid Lennox over the past weeks, she'd often spied the two brothers together, training the men, heading out on patrol, or talking together on the wall. Lennox got on well with Kerr and Brodie, yet she'd also noted the easy rapport between him and Iver when she'd seen them talking at mealtimes. There had been a rift of sorts between them before, and she was pleased to see it healed.

"I've still got those recruits to train," Lennox added then, his smile fading. "The warriors of Dun Ugadale need to be fighting fit, just in case we are called to fight for the crown in the coming months." He grimaced. "And relations between the MacAlisters and the MacDonalds grow sourer with each passing month. We could have problems with them in the future."

Davina nodded. "Growing up, my father told me there's always trouble of some sort to contend with. Peace and prosperity are hard won and easily lost."

"Aye," Lennox replied. "He's not wrong." His thumb skimmed across her lower lip. "But tonight, trouble lies elsewhere, lass. Tonight, all that exists is us."

EPILOGUE: LEGACY

Two months later ...

"DO YE NOT like my guise, Davina?"

"No ... ye look like an evil crow."

Lennox snorted a laugh. "That's what Iver said when I wore something similar at Stirling."

Arms folded across her chest, Davina eyed her husband. They were both guised for Samhuinn and would shortly join the inhabitants of the broch and the villagers and farmers who lived around Dun Ugadale, upon a nearby hill, where the bonfire would be lit.

Davina had donned a black cloak and the mask of a crone. It wasn't a pretty guise, yet Lennox's was worse. He was dressed in black leather, a black feathered mask with a wicked beak protruding.

"Ye will frighten bairns," she pointed out.

"And so will ye, wife," he replied, a smile in his voice. "Dressed as the Bean-Nighe. Shall we go down and see how many we can send running to their mother's skirts?"

Davina gave an exasperated sigh, even as a smile tugged at her mouth. "Ye, Lennox Mackay, are incorrigible."

"One of the many reasons ye love me." He then hooked an arm through Davina's, steering her toward the door of their chamber. "Come, angel, or they'll have run out of soul cakes and wassail by the time we arrive."

They left the tower, descending to the lower levels of the broch, and then emerging into the barmkin beyond. The yard that surrounded the broch, separating it from the walls, was empty; as Lennox had predicted, everyone had gone out to watch the lighting of the fire.

Night had fallen, the sky a carpet of sparkling stars overhead, and the scent of woodsmoke lay heavy in the air. And when they passed through the gate and walked down to the village, Davina's gaze alighted upon the great fire that burned upon a hill to the north.

It glowed like a beacon, its golden light warming the sky. Around its base, she spied the silhouettes of dancing figures.

Arm-in-arm, they took the winding path through the village. Bairns ran past, dressed as brownies, their squeals of delight lifting high into the air. And as they climbed the hill to the bonfire, Davina's gaze slid over men and women guised as wulvers, selkies, and various other mythical creatures.

They joined the laird and his wife. Iver had painted his face in woad and wore blue. He'd also draped seaweed over his shoulders and through his hair, to make himself look like one of the Blue Men of Minch, blue-skinned 'storm kelpies' who were said to sink boats and drown sailors. Next to him, Bonnie was clad as a forest sprite. She wore an emerald surcoat and pine-green cloak and had woven foliage through her hair.

"Mother Mary," Bonnie greeted them, her eyebrows arching. "Ye two make a fine pair."

"Isn't that the same mask ye wore for the masquerade ball in Stirling?" Iver asked Lennox, screwing his face up in distaste.

"No, but I did my best to replicate it," Lennox quipped, his mouth tugging into a grin underneath the jutting beak.

"A fine guise indeed, brother," rumbled a familiar voice. Davina turned to see a broad-shouldered figure standing behind them. A ram's skull covered Brodie's face, yet she recognized his brawn. Next to him, Kerr was shrouded in seal skin, his pale hair gleaming in the firelight. Davina grinned. Unlike his terrifying-looking brothers, Kerr cut a handsome figure, this eve. He made a fine selkie, indeed.

Around them, the festivities were already well underway. Local women were carrying baskets of sweet, soft cakes studded with dried blackcurrants, which they shared with the hungry revelers. Meanwhile, farmers' wives ladled out cups of wassail, mulled apple cider.

"Is that really ye under there, Davina?" Bonnie asked, stepping close to inspect the mask that Davina had fashioned out of glue and crushed oats before painting it.

"Aye." Davina reached up and touched the hideous visage she'd crafted. "The Washerwoman isn't supposed to be pretty."

Indeed, the Bean-Nighe was hideous, and if one sighted the hag washing clothes by a river, it was an omen of death.

A young woman approached them, bearing a basket of fragrant soul cakes. Tall, with a voluptuous figure and walnut-colored hair cascading over her shoulders, Rose MacAlister was dressed like a Sidhe maiden, with pointed ears and a crown of ivy.

Davina was sure the lass didn't realize to whom she was bringing cakes until she halted before them. Her smile then wavered, and her gaze hardened.

Wordlessly, she held out the basket.

"Thank ye, lass," Iver said, helping himself to a cake.

"These smell delicious," Lennox added, taking two for himself.

"I baked them myself," she replied stiffly. "It was my mother's recipe."

Davina watched Rose with interest. Her relationship with the Mackays was a strained one. After all, the laird had struck off her father's right hand after his repeated sheep and cattle thieving. However, she wasn't foolish enough to be rude to Iver Mackay and his wife.

Kerr stepped forward then, reaching out to help himself to a cake, but Rose abruptly turned away and walked off.

Brow furrowing, Kerr dropped his hand to his side.

"Rose doesn't like ye much, does she?" Brodie murmured, amused.

Kerr grunted as if he couldn't care less. Nonetheless, Davina marked how his frown didn't ease, and how his gaze tracked Rose as she walked away. Although she'd never remarked on it to anyone, Davina hadn't forgotten how he'd stared at the lass in the kirk months earlier.

Judging from his lingering gaze now, Rose still fascinated him.

"I'm glad yer father joined us for Samhuinn," Bonnie said then, drawing Davina's attention. "Although I'm not sure Sheena agrees."

Davina's attention shifted across the crowd to where Colin Campbell stood, resplendent in a deerskin cloak and antlers. Cup of wassail in hand, he loomed over Sheena, while she listened to him, tight-lipped with irritation.

Unlike most folk, Davina's mother-by-marriage hadn't donned a guise for the occasion. Instead, she wore a shimmering grey cloak, her pale hair swept high. When Davina suggested she help her make a Samhuinn costume, Sheena had snorted. "Such nonsense is for the young."

Sheena and Davina's relationship had deepened to a friendship of sorts of late, especially while Bonnie and Iver had been away recently. They'd gone north to Castle Varrich, delivering Dun Ugadale's taxes personally, and had been hosted by the Mackay clan-chief himself.

"She suffers my father surprisingly well," Davina replied, her mouth quirking.

Bonnie laughed. The two women moved closer, while their menfolk walked off, in search of some mulled cider. They watched the revelry for a few moments before Bonnie sighed. "I wish Niel and Beth Mackay could have attended as well."

Davina cut her friend a surprised look. "Did ye invite the clan-chief here?"

Bonnie nodded. "I was nervous about meeting him," she admitted, "but he and his wife made me very welcome at Varrich. I met many others of the clan too, as well as some of the Mackay allies." She paused then, her mouth curving once more. "And I made a new friend."

Davina inclined her head. "Aye?"

"A lass called Greer … she's the Forbes clan-chief's daughter. She's a little younger than us, although she has a way about her that lights up even the dreariest day. Ye'd love her."

Davina smiled at this description. "I'm sure I would, for ye are a good judge of character."

"I invited her to join us for Samhuinn as well, but she couldn't attend." The disappointment in Bonnie's voice was evident.

"Well, ye must invite her to stay with us in the spring," Davina replied firmly. Like Bonnie, she was keen to meet other women, to widen their circle of acquaintance. It could feel isolated at times down here on the Kintyre peninsula.

"Mulled cider for ye both?"

Davina turned to find her husband standing behind them, two steaming cups of wassail held aloft.

"Thank ye, my love," she replied, taking the cups, and handing one to Bonnie.

Meanwhile, Iver had returned to his wife's side. He murmured something to her, and Lady Mackay laughed, the warm sound carrying through the crowd.

Davina moved closer to her own husband, lifting up her mask so she could take a sip of her drink. The warmed, spiced cider burned down her throat, and she sighed. She then linked her arm through Lennox's, leaning against him.

"I have news," he murmured then, dipping his head close, careful not to stab her with his beak.

Davina glanced up at him. "Aye?"

"Do ye remember what ye said on our wedding night, about us having land and a broch of our own one day?"

Her stomach fluttered, and she nodded.

"Well, Iver has just confirmed that we may have a parcel of land that runs alongside the western shore of Lussa Loch, inland from here."

Davina's breathing grew shallow. "Truly?"

Lennox's mouth kicked into a wide smile under his beak. "Truly. It's good sheep grazing country … and we can build a broch on the loch's edge. What do ye think?"

Davina squealed with excitement and threw herself into his arms. Wassail sloshed over the edge of her cup, but she paid it no mind.

She and Lennox hadn't spoken of her idea since their wedding, and she'd thought he'd forgotten. But he hadn't.

He'd remembered and had been working toward obtaining the land. For her. For them.

Reaching up, she pushed up his feathered and beaked mask onto the crown of his head so she could see her husband's face. He was gazing down at her, his dark-blue eyes expectant.

"I think ye have done well," she replied huskily.

"I know ye want a household of yer own, lass … and I too want us to have our independence."

She nodded, warmth suffusing her chest. They both enjoyed their lives at Dun Ugadale, yet they were too independent in spirit to remain here forever. Davina longed to build something with her husband, a legacy they could leave behind them.

"Such news deserves a kiss," she said, smiling.

He grinned back. "Go on then."

Looping her free arm around his neck, Davina raised her chin and leaned in, capturing his mouth with hers. And there, amongst the Samhuinn revelry, she kissed him deeply, for all to see.

The End

HISTORICAL NOTES

This story is set around the reign of James II of Scotland. James ruled from 1430 to 1460. During this period, James was locked in civil strife with the Douglases (if you've read Book One in this series, you'll know all about that!).

After the murder of William Douglas by the king—when the earl refused to break his alliance with two powerful Highland clan-chiefs—the Douglas clan marched on Stirling with the letters of safe conduct pinned to a horse's tail and disavowed their oath to James.

The months of conflict that followed (the time in which this novel takes place) were tantamount to civil war. James II kept hold of the Crown and the Stewart dynasty would continue. In the aftermath of William's murder, James set out to remove the Douglas's power from Scotland, resulting in the family's ultimate destruction in 1455.

HIGHLANDER HONORED begins at Kilchurn Castle. This castle was built by Colin Campbell (our heroine's father). The first castle comprised the five-floor tower house, with a courtyard defended by an outer wall. At the time, Kilchurn was on a small island scarcely larger than the castle itself—at the northeastern end of Loch Awe—and would have been accessed via an underwater or low-lying causeway.

Later, we move on to Iona Abbey, the ruins of which still stand on the Isle of Iona, next to the island of Mull, off the western coast of Scotland. The abbey is one of the oldest Christian religious centers in Western Europe and was a focal point for the spread of Christianity throughout Scotland. Such nunneries only admitted wealthy women, and dowries were expected. As such,

Davina's lack of one would have been considered a real problem. There was an abbess named Anna at Iona during the 15th Century, and she was reputed to have two small pet dogs. I used her as inspiration for the abbess in my story!

The stronghold of Dun Ugadale is an iron age fort on the promontory near Ugadale on the Kintyre peninsula. Although it's now a ruin, the fort was owned by the Mackays from the 14th century and was passed through marriage in the 17th century to the MacNiels.

REBELLIOUS HIGHLAND HEARTS CHARACTER GLOSSARY

Main characters

Davina Campbell (Colin Campbell's daughter)
Lennox Mackay (Captain of the Kilchurn Guard)

Other characters

Abbess Anna (abbess at Iona Abbey)
Athol MacNab (steward of Kilchurn)
Bonnie Mackay (Iver's wife)
Brodie Mackay (blacksmith at Dun Ugadale)
Brogan Douglas (cousin to the 9th Earl of Douglas)
Colin Campbell (the Lord of Glenorchy)
Cory (cook at Dun Ugadale)
Father Ross (priest at Dun Ugadale)
Graham MacAlister (farmer at Dun Ugadale)
Hamish, Keith, Archie, Fergus, and Elliot (Kilchurn guards)
Iver Mackay (Mackay chieftain—laird of Dun Ugadale)
Kerr Mackay (Captain of the Dun Ugadale Guard)
Kyle MacAllister (bailiff at Dun Ugadale)
Rose MacAlister (Graham MacAlister's daughter)
Sheena Mackay (mother to Iver, Lennox, and Kerr)

ABOUT THE AUTHOR

Multi-award-winning author Jayne Castel writes epic Historical and Fantasy Romance. Her vibrant characters, richly researched historical settings, and action-packed adventure romance transport readers to forgotten times and imaginary worlds.

Jayne is the author of a number of best-selling series. In love with all things Scottish, she writes romances set in both Dark Ages and Medieval Scotland.

When she's not writing, Jayne is reading (and re-reading) her favorite authors, cooking Italian feasts, and going on long walks with her husband. She lives in New Zealand's beautiful South Island.

Connect with Jayne online:
www.jaynecastel.com
www.facebook.com/JayneCastelRomance
https://www.instagram.com/jaynecastelauthor/
Email: contact@jaynecastel.com

Printed in Great Britain
by Amazon

25486447R10139